DEEP STATE

A NATHANIEL CADE STORY

CHRISTOPHER
FARNSWORTH

DEEP STATE
A Nathaniel Cade Story
Copyright © 2017 by Christopher Farnsworth

Printed in the USA.

Cover Design and Interior Format
© THE KILLION GROUP INC.

ALSO BY
CHRISTOPHER FARNSWORTH

FLASHMOB

KILLFILE

THE ETERNAL WORLD

THE BURNING MEN

RED, WHITE, AND BLOOD

THE PRESIDENT'S VAMPIRE

BLOOD OATH

*To everyone who would not let
Cade go quietly into the night.*

T HIS MUCH IS TRUE....

In 1867, a young sailor was tried and convicted of murdering two of his crew mates and drinking their blood.

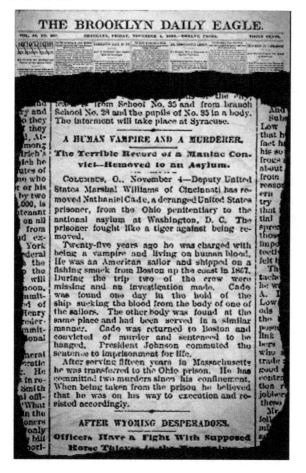

THE BROOKLYN DAILY EAGLE.

...from School No. 35 and from branch School No. 28 and the pupils of No. 35 in a body. The interment will take place at Syracuse.

A HUMAN VAMPIRE AND A MURDERER.

The Terrible Record of a Maniac Convict—Removed to an Asylum.

COLUMBUS, O., November 4—Deputy United States Marshal Williams of Cincinnati has removed Nathaniel Cade, a deranged United States prisoner, from the Ohio penitentiary to the national asylum at Washington, D. C. The prisoner fought like a tiger against being removed.

Twenty-five years ago he was charged with being a vampire and living on human blood. He was an American sailor and shipped on a fishing smack from Boston up the coast in 1867. During the trip two of the crew were missing and an investigation made. Cade was found one day in the hold of the ship sucking the blood from the body of one of the sailors. The other body was found at the same place and had been served in a similar manner. Cade was returned to Boston and convicted of murder and sentenced to be hanged. President Johnson commuted the sentence to imprisonment for life.

After serving fifteen years in Massachusetts he was transferred to the Ohio prison. He has committed two murders since his confinement. When being taken from the prison he believed that he was on his way to execution and resisted accordingly.

AFTER WYOMING DESPERADOES.

Officers Have a Fight With Supposed Horse Thieves...

The papers called him a vampire.

President Andrew Johnson pardoned him, sparing his life. He spent the rest of his days in an asylum for the criminally insane.

At least, that was the cover story.

The truth was far stranger. The young man, named Nathaniel Cade, was actually a vampire. Bound by a special blood oath, he swore to follow the orders of the President of the United States and protect the nation from the forces of darkness that cannot ever be allowed to invade the daylight world of ordinary humans. For over 145 years, Cade has been a secret weapon in the war against the Other Side, both the first responder and the last line of defense.

Zach Barrows was a young political operative with a bright future on his way to becoming the youngest chief of staff in White House history. Then he was called into the Oval Office and given a much different assignment. Zach became the latest in a long line of human handlers to work with Cade. Zach thought it was all a bad joke until he met the vampire in the flesh; then he wet his pants. Things have only slightly improved for him since then.

The two may appear close in age, but Cade is an inhuman, blood-drinking monster. Zach is an ambitious political creature. They are worlds apart, but have managed to forge a grudging respect since Zach's first mission. Zach now uses his intellect and resources to do the things in the daylight world that Cade cannot. He relays the president's orders and deals with all the logistics necessary to keep Cade hidden in a world that's increasingly hostile to secrets.

And Cade kills the monsters.

"WE ALL KNOW THE EARTH is in trouble. We have now entered into 6X — the sixth major extinction of life on this planet. I have often wondered if there was a United Organization of Organisms… and every organism had a right to vote, would we be voted on the planet, or off the planet?"

— *Paul Stamets*

CHAPTER ONE

PARKER, WYOMING. YESTERDAY.

FOR SOME REASON, CAPTAIN RICHARD Braden could not get the song out of his head. *"We built this city on rock and roll..."*

It had come up randomly on the radio as he parked, just before he killed the car engine. That was a full day and over 2,000 miles away, but the song was still bouncing around madly inside his skull.

It was driving him nuts. He'd been trained to endure torture, think clearly under enemy fire, and disarm a suitcase nuke, but the sheer idiocy of this one bad 80s hit was now thoroughly kicking his ass.

For starters, why was Marconi playing the mamba? The mamba is a snake, not a song. Even if they meant the mambo, that was a dance, not a song. Just how stoned were they when they wrote this piece of crap anyway?

He shook it off and focused on the task at hand. Braden was moving into the perimeter of the town, dark and as quiet as a shadow, his H&K MP7a1 off-safety and ready to fire.

Braden was a member of SEAL Team Gold, one of the U.S government's most secret warriors, ordinarily charged with hunting down international terrorists or rescuing hostages held in deep enemy territory.

Right now, Braden was about to recon a 24-hour convenience store on the edge of Parker, Wyoming.

Parker was a small town — so small, in fact, that the convenience store wasn't even a 7-11 or a Circle K, but some local equivalent called a "Go-Fer Mart." Population: 308. Local industry: ranching, with some oil money from active wells nearby. One church, one bar. Zero McDonalds. Parker seemed as innocuous as small-town America could get.

Braden didn't see anything to contradict that first impression. Instead, he saw a bored kid behind a counter, wearing a polyester vest and a nametag, waiting around on the off-chance that somebody wanted to buy beef jerky or beer at one in the morning.

But Braden had also been trained to observe his own responses, to run constant self-diagnostics, while on a mission. And he recognized that the nagging repetition of the crappy pop song in his head was a signal from his subconscious. It told him that something was wrong.

It wasn't just that Gold wasn't supposed to do domestic operations — this was hardly his first covert op on U.S. soil. Nor did he think he and the other team members had been called out for a false alarm. Braden had seen some seriously upfucked intel before, but this was a whole different flavor of weird.

Everything looked normal, but it wasn't. He couldn't say why. That's why the song was yammering in his head. It was like an alarm bell going off.

But try as he might, Braden couldn't see what he was missing.

He clicked his mike once, letting his team leader know he was in position. He received two clicks back, telling him to stay put.

Braden and the other five members of Gold had been mobilized early that morning. They flew across country in a troop transport, got loaded into a chopper at the Natrona County airport, then dropped at the edge of the highway, roughly three miles away from the town center. Nobody spotted them. The town was dead. There was zero traffic. Braden figured it wasn't much of a tourist destination.

Based on the mission briefing, Braden expected to deal with some militia retards. There were still a few McVeigh types out here, looking to make a bigger bang than Oklahoma City. He wasn't worried about those morons. For all their talk about resistance and death before dishonor, he suspected it would be a race to see what they'd do first: drop their weapons or shit their pants.

But it never hurt to be prepared. That was why he was spotting the Kwik-E-Mart here. There wasn't much in the way of high ground in Parker, so Braden would set up a sniper post on the roof, ready to fill some graves if necessary.

The team leader's voice came over his earbud. "We're in position. Braden, how's it look?"

He responded through his own throat-mike. "One civilian. Other than that, zero contacts."

"Let's go," the team leader said. "Quick and quiet."

Braden moved. He ran fast to the rear door of the convenience store. He used a pick gun to pop the lock, and was inside before the kid would have a chance to wonder about the slight noise.

He passed the restroom and a small office, the layout of the place already fixed in his mind from his brief surveillance. With three long strides, he was at the counter, his arm around the kid's throat, dragging him back, out of sight of the big glass windows.

He put the kid down hard, one gloved hand over his mouth.

"Quiet," he ordered. "Bad news is, you make a sound, I'll have to shoot you. Good news is, we're the good guys."

The kid stared back at him, eyes only mildly curious.

Braden took his hand away. The kid didn't speak.

"Hey. You all right?"

Still nothing. Just the wide, placid eyes. Christ, Braden thought, the local pot must be something else.

"Listen. We're here to help. I'm not going to hurt you," Braden said.

That finally seemed to get through to the kid. He started to smile.

"I know," he said.

The song was almost screaming in Braden's head now.

The kid opened his mouth in a full grin.

Braden was up and on his feet and running out the back door before he even realized it. He blew radio silence right to shit. He had to warn the others.

Jesus Christ, what was in that kid's mouth?

"Top, top!" he shouted into his mike. "We've got to run, we've got to get out of here — "

Gunfire. He knew the sound well. It was the suppressed report of another H&K MP7. The others were already under attack.

There was the flat, hollow boom of a combat shotgun, a hundred yards in the other direction, followed by a scream.

That was Turner. He recognized the voice, but just barely. He'd seen Turner break his arm during a training exercise, a compound fracture, the bone tearing up through the skin. Turner had only grunted then. Now he was screaming like a child.

He kept running, checking over his shoulder. The convenience store glowed in the night. The kid wasn't coming after him.

Braden didn't think that meant he was safe.

"Top, call it in!" he shouted into his mike. The team leader had a sat-phone. He had to tell them. Had to warn someone.

More gunfire, then abrupt silence in the distance. Not even a scream this time. His earbud was filled with nothing but static.

They were dead. They were all dead.

He kept running.

Something came from behind and spun him about. There was a pain in his chest, but he could not feel his legs. He found himself on his back, looking at the stars.

Then something blotted them out, and Braden felt nothing at all.

CHAPTER TWO

OMAHA, NEBRASKA. TODAY.

ZACH BARROWS SAT AT HIS desk, listening to the man drone on.

"So, you see, it all comes back to the Nordics. They made an agreement with the Greys after the crash at Roswell. That was the first time they had to really deal with humans. Of course, they were monitoring our nuclear program at Los Alamos, but they hadn't counted on our primitive atomic testing to interfere with their ion drives. So they were forced to barter for new technology with the Nordics, who'd already compensated for that, because they'd given us the atomic bomb in the first place…"

Zach had already forgotten the man's name. He'd written it down, of course. It was somewhere on one of the many forms in front of him. He was required to record every detail of every one of these conversations. Every piece of paper he filled out was then checked by a whole team of bureaucrats, each one just itching for the chance to mark a misspelled word and send the whole mess back to him.

Zach would not say this was Hell — he'd seen the real thing, and this was not even close — but it was definitely Purgatory. Hell, for all its faults, at least was not this boring.

This was his job now. Any person who called the FBI or the Air Force or the post office with a story of seeing Bigfoot or a UFO or the Jersey Devil was shuffled along a chain of command that eventually reached Zach, and his tiny closet of an office in a gray federal building in Omaha. Zach was then required to take a detailed account of each case of body-cavity probing, ape-human hybridization, and/or Satanic conspiracy. He was the U.S. government's sole public response to every case of paranormal activity in the country.

So now he spent eight hours a day — he could be punished by an administrative letter in his file if he took unauthorized overtime — listening to lunatics who were convinced that they alone knew the true shape of the world, that they alone saw the monsters hidden in the shadows.

They had no idea.

He'd been assigned to Omaha after being bounced from his old job by President Lester Wyman himself, the 45th occupant of the Oval Office.

Zach could kill him for this.

Well. Among other reasons.

He dragged his attention back to the man, who was really excited, almost hopping up and down in his chair.

"And *this* is where it gets really interesting. In

order to protect that trade agreement with the Galactic Senate — you understand, that's just the human term for it, I'm approximating here, of course — they were forced to find another president who'd be more amenable to providing them with human children. That was why they recruited Lee Harvey Oswald, and cloned him. Now, this is where it gets tricky, so bear with me…"

Zach restrained a yawn and sneaked a look at the time on his desktop monitor. 10:33. Unbelievable. It felt like time had stopped.

"Why do you think they care?" Zach found himself asking.

The man stopped. Blinked. He wasn't used to people actually speaking to him, Zach could tell.

"What?"

"The aliens," Zach said. "I just see one big problem in this whole story of yours. What makes you think they care what happens to us?"

The man's eyes narrowed. He scowled, but there was a little satisfaction in his expression as well.

"You don't believe me," he said. "That's fine. I'm used to this kind of petty, narrow-minded bigotry from government functionaries like yourself — "

Zach cut him off. "No, no," Zach said. "You're right. There are aliens. You're absolutely right about that."

The man stopped. Opened his mouth to speak. Closed it again.

"Never thought you'd hear anyone admit it, did you?" Zach said. "Well. It's true. Do you want me to let you in on another little secret?"

He leaned over the desk and lowered his voice. The man leaned in too, eyes wide.

"They do not give a shit about us," Zach whispered. "They look at us the way we look at amoebas under a microscope. They barely register our sad little planet's existence. And they're content to let us keep killing each other until we go extinct."

The man blinked. Sat back.

Zach nodded. "We're not alone. But we might as well be."

The man's chin trembled, for just a second. Then the defiant look returned. "You're lying," he said.

Zach shrugged. "I wish I was."

The man stood. Without another word, he gathered his stack of folders filled with evidence meticulously downloaded from the Internet, and left.

Zach sighed. This one had looked so normal when he'd come in. Zach had allowed himself a brief moment of hope that he might have something authentic. He wore a suit, he'd showered recently, had no dandruff on his shoulders — but within five minutes of his spiel, Zach knew he was utterly delusional.

For starters, there had never been a UFO crash at Roswell. It was at Dulce. Zach had seen the corpse himself.

In a hidden basement of the Smithsonian. In his old job.

When he'd been the keeper of the President's Vampire.

When he fought real demons. Killed monsters. Kept the people in the daylight safe from the things in the dark.

But that was then.

Now he had an empty coffee cup and a meeting

scheduled in fifteen minutes with another delusional paranoid.

He could fix one of those things. He got up for
more coffee. And tried not to think about the time
when he actually saved lives, and how it ended.

CHAPTER THREE

WASHINGTON, D.C. FOUR YEARS AGO.

ZACH AND CADE WERE CALLED to the Oval Office before President Samuel Curtis' body was even buried.

Lester Wyman had taken the oath of office while flying back to Washington D.C. Cade had felt it when the power transferred. It was part of his own oath. His loyalty switched to the new president. Just like that.

But it didn't change the fact that he and Zach both loathed the man.

They stood before Wyman at what had been, just 24 hours earlier, the desk of Samuel Curtis.

Zach was still in shock then. He'd worked for Curtis since high school, joining his campaign as a volunteer and rising to become one of his most trusted aides. He'd loved Curtis more than his own father, who'd also died in the previous month. But he wasn't numb. All the pain and anger and grief had curdled inside him and formed a ball of pure hate.

Cade — well, it was hard to tell how Cade felt. Because Cade was an honest-to-God vampire, and as Zach had learned, vampires are not the most emotionally available creatures.

Cade did not look particularly terrifying in context. He sat there, just like any other government operative in a cheap suit. He looked lean and hard, but you might write that off to regular Crossfit sessions.

But there was an almost palpable sense of menace that hung over him. For Zach it felt very much like looking at a Great White Shark behind glass at an aquarium — except in this case the shark, if it wanted to, could break down the barrier at any time for lunch. People felt uneasy around Cade without knowing why. Some basic survival instinct in the back of their brains began screaming, telling them to get away.

Zach had thought he was being pranked when they first met. A vampire. Right. Then he saw the fangs.

Since that first meeting, Zach discovered that Cade was the real thing. Immortal, inhumanly fast and strong, and only one of many creatures of the night that existed in real life. He was also the only one on their side. In 1867, Cade was discovered on a ship that ran aground in Boston Harbor and was bound by a special blood oath to follow the orders of the President of the United States. He was the country's first response and the last line of defense against everything that waited in the dark.

Zach learned later that Cade did not drink human blood. He stuck to animal blood, although it made him weaker — like filling a Maserati with cheap kerosene instead of high-test unleaded. This wasn't part of his oath. It was a personal choice, like the rough metal cross he wore around his neck. He had faith, even though he did not believe he would ever be saved.

Zach was just the latest in a line of human handlers who did the daylight chores for the vampire. Together, they had faced soldiers reanimated from the corpses of the dead, reptilian-human hybrids that spread their mutation like a disease, men with the ability to turn their bodies into living bombs, covert operatives who worked for sinister forces, and, during the campaign, an unkillable serial killer who was stalking the president.

They'd beaten him, though not without cost. They'd saved the president's life.

And then he died in a room alone with Wyman.

Both Zach and Cade were certain Wyman was responsible for Curtis' death. They had no evidence, no proof. They didn't even have enough for an educated guess. All they had was their knowledge of the man.

That was enough.

Wyman didn't care much for them, either. Even newly wreathed in the power of the presidency, Zach could almost see it coming off him in waves — his pure contempt, and his rock-solid certainty that he now had them at his mercy.

Zach hated him even more at that moment, because he was right.

Cade was bound by his oath to follow any constitutional order of the president and his appointed officers or die trying. It was the leash that had been around his throat ever since he'd been found, the only way he'd ever been trusted to do his job. That Cade was a uniquely moral creature didn't matter to most of the men in the White House. All they really knew was that they had a vampire of their own, and he had to do what they told him.

Zach, on the other hand, was just along for the ride.

Wyman started on them right away.

"What? No congratulations?" he said, smirking.

Cade and Zach remained silent. Zach had several replies come to mind, but he didn't want to give Wyman the satisfaction.

"Well. I can't blame you, I suppose," Wyman said. "It is a solemn and grim time for our nation. We have lost a great man."

Zach clenched his fists so hard he thought his nails might draw blood.

"But our nation still needs protection. Which is why you are here. You did your best to keep the president safe. And even if he didn't protect his own health, you kept him alive."

Until we left him with you, Zach thought.

Cade's face, was, as always, impassive. Zach wondered how this little speech was going down with him. Probably not well.

Wyman paused. He looked at them both. The smirk came back.

"How do you feel about having to follow my orders now, Cade?" he asked.

"I don't," Cade said.

"You don't *what*?"

"I don't feel."

"That's not what I meant," Wyman said. "I prefer you to call me sir, like you did my predecessor."

"Yes sir."

Wyman smiled. "Much better. Let me put it another way. What would you do if I gave you an order you disagreed with?"

"As long as your order is lawful and constitutional and within the bounds of my oath, I am required to follow it. Sir."

"Right. So if I told you to kill Mr. Barrows right now?"

Zach's stomach flipped.

Cade didn't move, however. "I assume you wouldn't give such an order, sir. Since it would not be lawful. Zach has done nothing to warrant execution. What's more, he is under my protection as one of your sworn and appointed officers."

Wyman glared at Cade.

"Sir," Cade said.

"I see," Wyman said, frowning. He'd always had a very bad habit, for a politician, of letting his irritation show when he didn't get what he wanted. "Well, that's not actually the case anymore."

"What?" Zach said.

"As of this moment, you are no longer Cade's handler, Mr. Barrows," Wyman said. "Frankly, as I've watched your performance, I've seen that you put your own interests ahead of the nation's. That's not a quality we can afford in a man who's right next to one of our greatest weapons. I have another position in mind for you."

"And if I don't take it?" Zach said. "I think maybe it's time for me to go back to the private sector."

"You don't have a choice," Wyman snapped. "Your appointment was for a lifetime — one way or another. That doesn't change just because you're not working with Cade anymore. Believe me, you'll still be dealing with the same problems. But not with Cade. Not anymore."

"What if I quit anyway?"

"Then you can spend the rest of your natural life in a cell. We can't have someone with your knowledge walking around loose."

Zach looked at Wyman, then at Cade. Cade gave the smallest possible shrug of his shoulders. Which Zach knew meant that Wyman could do it. Cade wouldn't harm him, but if Wyman ordered him to track Zach down as a threat to national security, then Zach would be on his way to a black site before morning.

"Fine," Zach said. "Just happy to be on the team. Sir."

Wyman gave him a glittering smile. "Excellent," he said. "There was one other thing I needed to discuss with you both this morning. I have a lot to do. A country to run, you know. But I never agreed with Sam's decision not to use the weapons in the Reliquary."

That was an understatement. The Reliquary was a secret chamber under the Smithsonian that Cade used as a living space and a trophy room. In 145 years of fighting the Other Side, Cade had collected hundreds of occult objects that carried a little bit of the darkness with them. There were the stuffed bodies of impossible animals, the autopsied corpses of aliens and monsters, the shrapnel and wreckage of a hidden war. Things that could be used as tools and weapons. Keys that opened doors that should always remain closed.

President Curtis had seen the danger they represented. He had vetoed every attempt to bring the relics out of storage. But Wyman had looked at all those cursed objects and saw only power. Now he finally saw his chance to use them.

"So before you go, I will need an inventory of everything down in your little hidey-hole, Barrows. Plus a listing of each object's capabilities. I assume you've done some basic record-keeping," he said.

Zach almost felt like smiling. Wyman noticed the change immediately.

"What? What is it?"

"There is an inventory," Zach said. "But I'm afraid it won't do you much good."

"What? Why not?"

Cade didn't speak. Zach was happy to fill the silence.

"I am afraid that Cade reacted badly to the news of the president's death."

"What does that mean?"

"He destroyed much of the Reliquary last night."

Wyman's eyes went wide. His mouth dropped open.

"I apologize, sir," Cade said. "I am afraid that Zach is correct. I lost control of myself due to the death of a president on my watch. Roughly sixty percent of the artifacts housed in the main area of the Reliquary were destroyed. By me. Sir."

"You unbelievable blood-sucking bastard," Wyman hissed. "What have you done?"

Zach had to look down to keep from grinning. He didn't want Cade to be punished, and Wyman was clearly ready to explode at the slightest provocation.

But he had to admire Cade's foresight. He'd thought Cade was simply angry. Now he'd be willing to bet that the vampire had very carefully targeted only the most dangerous things in the Reliquary in his rampage. Now they would never get out into the world again.

"You said you don't *feel*," Wyman said, through gritted teeth.

"As you said, sir. President Curtis was a great man. We all mourn his loss in our own way."

Wyman sat back in his chair. He took a deep breath. Sat up straight and tried to look presidential.

"Get out," he said.

They both turned to go.

"Just you, Barrows," Wyman said. "You can get your new assignment from my assistant. Cade, you will remain here. I'm not done with you yet."

Zach looked back at Cade. Cade nodded his head slightly, and then faced Wyman again.

"Well?" Wyman said. "You waiting for a hug? Go."

Zach walked out of the Oval Office. Wyman's assistant gave him a packet with his new instructions and a plane ticket to Omaha.

Then he left the White House.

He hadn't seen Cade since.

CHAPTER FOUR

THE EMIRATE OF DUBAI. TODAY.

NATHANIEL CADE STOOD OUTSIDE A worker's camp on the outskirts of the desert near Dubai. He was a little more than an hour by car from the glittering city and its gleaming sky-scrapers on the edge of the Persian Gulf. The sky above was dark.

Sunrise was three hours away. More than enough time.

He began walking toward the razor-wire fence at the edge of the highway. If anyone were to pass by, they might wonder why the fence was angled inward at the top, as if to keep people from climb-ing out rather than getting in. They might wonder why a small group of buildings in the middle of nowhere would even need a locked fence.

Cade didn't. He'd seen the thing that had escaped recently.

It made its way to the gulf by sheer luck, mostly blind and hideously deformed, before it died on the shore. A tourist on a boat tour came ashore to take a piss and got a picture of the decomposing corpse. Its picture was briefly famous as some kind of a sea monster. It was passed around Facebook and Twitter before one of the government's friendly scientists defused the whole situation by identifying it as the rotted husk of a dead basking shark.

Cade knew what it really was, however. He recognized the work.

That was why he was here.

He vaulted the 12-foot fence effortlessly, the way a normal man might step up onto a curb. He landed lightly, but not lightly enough to avoid setting off the motion detectors buried in the sand. Ears that heard in a range far beyond human picked up on the electronic whine of alarms inside the buildings ahead of him.

He didn't care. He was, in fact, looking forward to this part.

A door slammed open on the cinderblock building nearest Cade. The first soldiers came running out, night-vision goggles tracking the fence line. They wore black uniforms and full body armor. Each one also had chain-mail and ceramic plates wrapped around his neck.

So they'd heard he might be coming.

They dropped into firing formation, the first line of men taking a knee, spraying covering fire along the ground, sending a wave of bullets in Cade's direction, while the men behind them stood and aimed more carefully, looking for a specific target.

Cade accelerated. He moved through the bullets as if they were frozen in the air. Then he hit the men.

They broke into pieces, their blood spraying into mist as their limbs were torn from their bodies on impact with Cade. Cade watched for a split-second as the little red globes hung in front of him.

But he didn't stop. He still had to complete the mission.

He left the dead guards at the entrance and moved through the building, down a flight of stairs to the hidden chambers below.

Deep-scanning satellite imagery had revealed the complex under the camp. It went down for nearly a hundred feet into the sand and dirt.

Still moving faster than the human eye could see, he swept past the first lab and the cages there, where the workers were held. They'd been promised good jobs at good pay in Dubai, adding to the ever-shifting skyline, building another hotel or shopping mall for the richest people in the world.

Instead, they'd been drugged and delivered here. For the experiments.

Now the lucky ones were dead.

The unlucky ones looked at Cade through the Plexiglas walls of their holding cells. They were distorted, mutated, twisted into unnatural shapes. Most could not move under their own power any longer. Their bodies had become organ farms, breeding grounds for exotic bacteria or biological weapons, test beds for inimical combinations of genes.

Some detected Cade through senses grown painfully aware and acute. They shifted and called to him for help.

The ones who still had mouths to speak did, anyway.

Cade made them a silent promise to deliver mercy. But first. The target. The man who did this to them.

The guards who were inside the next level were smarter. They'd quickly rigged a series of grenades on a tripwire and hid behind a heavy door at the end of the first room.

Cade crawled along the ceiling, skittering like a roach, and avoided the trap altogether. He dropped down and yanked the door off its hinges.

The first guard stood gaping as the door came away from its frame. Cade punched a hole in his chest. He tore the throat from another with a flick of his wrist. He picked up the third guard and used him to bludgeon the fourth.

The fifth guard had clearly planned ahead. He did not have time to react once Cade hit the others. He must have been pressing the button on the suicide vest as soon as Cade appeared.

Cade heard the electricity sing along the wires in the vest, on its way to the blocks of plastic explosive strapped around the man's chest.

Cade was fast, but not faster than that.

So he kicked the last guard in the chest, sending him flying, putting as much distance between them as he possibly could.

He lifted the steel door and used it as a shield just as the explosives went off.

Cade waited for the smoke to clear. The explosion left his sensitive ears ringing. He stepped carefully through the doorway, expecting more gunfire.

Instead, he found a room full of bodies. The guards were in pieces all over the room, killed by the contained force of the explosion.

One final guard rushed into the chamber, firing a pistol.

It was more of a last, defiant gesture than anything else. Through the persistent ringing in his ears, Cade could hear the man cursing him in English, calling him an abomination, a demon, an obscenity.

Cade did not disagree with any of it.

He sidestepped the bullets, then crossed the distance between them. He lifted the guard off the floor with one hand, and used the other to tear away the headgear and the protective shields around his neck.

There, Cade found a cross on a chain.

He held the man dangling off the ground and looked at him. For a fraction of a second, something like a smile twitched across Cade's lips.

"That's right," the man gasped. He was American, unlike the rest of the soldiers, his voice accented with the inflections of prep school and the Ivy League. Blonde-haired and blue-eyed. "I know who you are. I know *what* you are."

"I should hope so," Cade said. He'd been hitting installations like this one for several years now, slaughtering every person and thing inside. He had not exactly been discreet.

"Yeah, well, I know you won't touch me. Not while I'm wearing this," the man said, flicking at the cross and sneering at Cade.

The arrogance and certainty brought the brief smile back to Cade's face. Something about these new recruits, who always assumed they were invulnerable.

"That might have been the case once," Cade said. "However, those conditions no longer apply."

Doubt appeared in the man's eyes. Then terror as Cade smiled and revealed his fangs.

Cade tore open the man's throat before he could scream, and drank the lifeblood from him.

He dropped the corpse, drained and empty, to the floor. There was a time he tried to fight his true nature. When he did not give into his thirst, no matter how much his enemies might have deserved it.

But he'd fallen off that wagon, and he saw no reason to get back on board.

"Had enough?" a cultured voice asked. "I wouldn't want to interrupt if you're still eating."

Cade looked up and saw his target. Dr. Johann Konrad. Also occasionally known as the Baron Von Frankenstein.

But that was centuries ago. Today he looked like any other well-dressed, well-groomed tech executive. He wore a sharp suit and a Patek Phillippe 5016G.

He was the man responsible for the experiments in the other room. Over his very long life, he'd committed all manner of sins against God, Nature and Man.

"I'm finished," Cade said. "And so are you."

Konrad affected a look of boredom. He did not seem the least bit afraid of Cade.

But Cade's hearing had recovered. He detected the quickening of Konrad's pulse. He smelled the slight tang of fear in his sweat.

Still, Cade gave him points for style. The last time they'd seen one another, Cade had been prepared to rip Konrad's head clean off his body. The scientist had tried to kill the president. Infuriatingly, Konrad had escaped and hired himself out to an international network of terrorists, skipping around the globe, designing bio-weapons that turned raw human material into nightmares. His latest employer, the one who'd outfitted him with this lab, was an organization that had mixed the occult with forbidden science and made a handsome profit from it since 1886.

Cade had wanted to end Konrad since they first met during World War II. He had sworn that the next time he saw the scientist, he would kill him.

Again, however, those conditions no longer applied.

"I'm here to bring you back to the United States," Cade said. "President Wyman has extended you a job offer. I suggest you take it."

Konrad smiled with genuine relief. Then laughed.

"You see, Cade? I told you. There will always be a need for my services."

"Get your things," Cade said. "We have a plane to catch."

Konrad tapped a finger at one corner of his mouth. "You missed a spot," he said. "I'd like to say I'm surprised at you. But it was predictable. The strong will *always* feed on the weak. It's the law of nature."

Cade didn't reply. Instead, he turned his back on Konrad and walked to the lab.

He had a promise to keep to Konrad's latest test subjects.

★★★

Two hours later, they were in a specially outfitted Gulfstream, its windows blocked against the sun, flying out of Dubai International. Konrad was sipping a well-aged Macallan. Cade was reading his latest orders, delivered by the pilot.

"Where are we going?" Konrad asked lazily. "Washington D.C., I assume? Dreary little city. But better than a hole in the desert. I suppose."

"You're going to D.C.," Cade said. "I have another destination."

"How sad for me," Konrad said, and then ignored Cade as he pulled a copy of the *Journal of Biological Chemistry* from his bag and began reading.

Cade, meanwhile, checked his watch. With the flight time, it would almost be sunset when he arrived in Omaha, Nebraska.

CHAPTER FIVE

OMAHA, NEBRASKA.

ZACH OPENED THE DOOR TO his one-bedroom apartment. He could afford something bigger or nicer — rents in Omaha were a quarter of what they were in D.C. — but he didn't need any more room. He had no social life, no friends, no casual acquaintances, even. The apartment was a place to keep his suits and to sleep: a closet with a bed.

He put his McDonalds bag on the counter of the tiny kitchen and began rummaging in a drawer.

"Hello, Zach."

Zach spun around, the gun already in his hand. He'd never stopped thinking Wyman would send someone for him someday. So he'd prepared.

He carried a Smith & Wesson Governor with him at all times. It was a specially chambered revolver designed to hold both .45 caliber bullets and .410 shotgun shells. It would stop pretty much anything on two feet.

Anything except the vampire currently standing

in the dark in his apartment.

"Jesus, Cade," Zach said, pointing the gun at the ceiling. "I could have shot you."

Cade gave him the ghost of a smile, as if it hadn't been almost four years. "No. You couldn't have."

"You don't know. I might have turned into a real gunslinger."

Cade just looked at him. Chatty as ever, Zach thought. Zach realized that Cade hadn't changed a bit. Which was not surprising, since he was, after all, a vampire. He didn't get older.

But it made Zach realize that he had. He and Cade had looked almost the same age when they first met. Now if they walked into a bar together, Cade would get carded, and Zach would not.

One more reminder — like the twinge in his knee lately or the gray hair he'd spotted in the mirror — that he had an expiration date, and Cade did not.

But there was something different about him, after all. It just took Zach a moment to notice it.

"Where's your cross?"

Zach touched his own throat. When he and Cade had worked together, Cade had always worn a rough metal cross around his neck on a leather cord. It burned him, like crosses burned all vampires, but Cade said the pain helped him focus. It kept his mind off his thirst for human blood.

Cade shifted slightly. Which told Zach he was uncomfortable. Cade rarely moved. He didn't fidget. He barely even breathed.

"I don't wear it anymore," Cade said.

"Right, I gathered that," Zach said. "Why not?"

Cade hesitated again. Zach got the feeling he had

somehow spoiled the big reunion.

"Things have changed since we worked together."

Zach decided to let it go at that. "Yeah. No kidding," he said. "So. You just dropped by to catch up?"

"We've been summoned."

"By Wyman?"

"Yes."

"He said I wasn't going to work with you anymore."

"Obviously, he's reconsidered."

"There's no way this is good news, is it?"

"For you or for me?"

"Funny, Cade. Real funny."

Again, the brief smile. For Cade, this was an unprecedented display of emotion. Like weeping and hugging.

"We should go," Cade said. "The plane is waiting." He looked at the paper sack on Zach's counter, the grease spots on its side. "You can bring your... dinner, I suppose."

"Oh right. Like you're a vegan."

Cade walked past Zach to the door and exited without another word.

Zach shook his head.

Just like old times.

"Yeah. Great to see you, too, Cade."

He took the burgers and followed.

CHAPTER SIX

WASHINGTON, D.C.

ZACH STOOD IN THE SITUATION Room below the White House. He stifled a yawn.

It had only taken a couple of hours to fly from Omaha to Andrews in the Gulfstream, and not much longer than that to get past the White House guards. But then Cade and Zach were kept waiting for hours. It was past midnight now.

Zach suspected Wyman was sleeping soundly somewhere upstairs in the residence, or was otherwise just keeping them waiting to screw with them. It was exactly the sort of amateur power move he'd expect from the former vice-president.

He was surprised how small everything seemed now, compared to how large this room loomed in his memories, and how it looked in photos or on TV.

Once upon a time, Zach would have been thrilled to be in one of the most secure locations on Earth, waiting for the President of the United States to outline a crisis.

Back then, Zach had been a political operator — one of the youngest staffers to work for President Samuel Curtis. He envisioned meetings like this as eventual chapters in his autobiography, where he'd describe how Curtis — with Zach's expert advice, of course — defused tensions on the Iranian border or forced Congress to pass some important piece of legislation.

Then he'd met Cade, and all those dreams plunged into nightmares like something out of a late-night horror movie. He'd helped save the world. Done more good than he ever could have as a politician.

And now he was bored out of his skull. He supposed he must be jaded, but there wasn't much of a thrill left in the Situation Room compared to seeing undead soldiers march through the Rose Garden.

He stood up, wandered around the room, drank coffee, looked at his phone (no signal, no surprise, since he was 40 feet below ground), sat down, then stood up again.

Cade, on the other hand, passed the time easily. He simply became more still, like a powered-down robot placed in one of the chairs at the small conference table.

Finally, at 12:43 a.m., the door opened, and President Lester Wyman entered, flanked by two Secret Service agents who eyed Cade and Zach with suspicion. They were on high alert, even in one of the most secure locations in the White House, Zach noticed. Wyman was spooked. He must have felt like there were enemies all around him.

Wyman didn't look well. The exhaustion was

plain on his face, and Zach decided he hadn't been sleeping after all. He didn't look like he'd slept well in a long, long time.

Living in the White House was like living on a planet with higher gravity. Zach had seen it age Curtis a decade in less than four years.

Wyman, not particularly handsome or youthful in the first place, was deteriorating even faster. Ever since he'd been described in one magazine as "a small, pale Smurf of a man," he'd started wearing makeup. It didn't help. The bronzer he applied every day gave a chemical orange cast to his skin. State meals and constant stress-eating had bloated him. He looked like a squat toadstool in a suit.

He'd won his first term in a landslide, riding a wave of sympathy from President Curtis' death less than two weeks before Election Day. The national spasm of grief put Wyman into office with a solid blue electoral map.

That was the last time anything went easily for him. Wyman wanted to separate himself from Curtis, to prove that he was his own man. So he began making big moves. He opened two new fronts in the War on Terror by sending troops into Syria and Yemen, which forced the military to fight in four active conflicts at once. He tried to bully China into more favorable trade agreements. He slashed the federal budget and shut down departments he thought were too expensive.

Today the military was stretched to its limits, soldiers were coming home in body bags, and there was talk of bringing back the draft. China's banks stopped buying U.S. debt and its government imposed taxes on everything American companies manufactured inside the country's borders. The financial markets tanked and unemployment doubled. Prices were up on everything and the shelves were barren at every Walmart in the country.

Predictably, people were not thrilled. Wyman was headed into his re-election campaign with his poll numbers at twenty-nine percent. And this time, he didn't have the sympathy vote.

Nobody felt sorry for Lester Wyman. Least of all Zach.

Cade stood to attention as Wyman entered. Zach was sure that was one of Wyman's orders. Zach sat down without being asked.

Wyman didn't notice. He sat and waited while one of the Secret Service agents got him a coffee — a breach of protocol there, the agents were not personal servants — then drank it quickly before he looked up at Cade and Zach.

"You may be seated," he told Cade. Cade sat, like an obedient dog. His face showed nothing, but Zach imagined there was a healthy bit of resentment stored behind the vampire's placid features. He had never taken well to being ordered around. Zach had learned that from personal experience.

"Barrows," Wyman said. "I'll skip the pleasantries, since we both know I'd be lying."

"Thanks, Les, I appreciate that."

The Secret Service goons bristled at Zach's tone. But Wyman didn't appear to care.

"I'll come right to the point. I need your help."

"No."

Wyman paused. "Excuse me?"

"No. Did I stutter?"

Wyman blinked, some of his drowsiness replaced

by irritation. "You haven't even heard what — "

"Don't know. Don't care. If you want my help, you called the wrong guy, because I am fresh out of fucks to give today."

Wyman sat up, his eyes finally taking on that snake-mean look that Zach remembered so well. He smiled, showing teeth. "Maybe I worded that badly, then, Zach. I assumed you were still a patriot. That you still had that much loyalty in you. That you'd be willing to answer when your president called."

God, Zach hated this guy.

"My president is dead," he said.

Wyman shook his head. "You don't think I'm legitimate? The country disagrees with you."

"Yeah, well. They don't know you like I do."

Wyman scowled. "Still such a smartass. Got an answer for everything. Cade has learned to work with me. Isn't that right, Cade?"

"Yes sir," Cade said. His voice was flat.

"You can order Cade around because of his oath. What are you going to do to me? Send me back to Omaha? I can deal with that."

"Let me tell you why you're here. Indulge me, before you go back to doing your important work in Nebraska."

Zach shrugged. "Fine. But there's nothing you can say that will — "

"We've lost all contact with a nuclear missile silo."

"Excuse me?" Zach said.

"Did I stutter?" Wyman snapped. "We lost contact with a manned nuclear silo outside Parker, Wyoming. The crew at this location goes down for 30-day stretches, with a regular check-in every 24 hours to receive the latest fail-safe codes. They failed to make the call yesterday."

Zach checked his watch. "What time was that?"

"Six a.m. MDT," Wyman said. "Start of the day shift."

Something bubbled up in Zach memory. He'd never been military, but he had a pretty good command of a lot of facts he'd learned in the course of his political career. That included the names and locations of every military base in the U.S. "We don't have a missile group in Parker, Wyoming," he said.

"Really," Wyman said, voice dripping with sarcasm. "You sure about that, Barrows? You think you know everything, just because you carried Cade's leash for a while? Or maybe you'll shut up for a moment and listen so I can tell you what happened."

Zach closed his mouth and did his best to put on his listening face.

Wyman grimaced and continued. "These are the phantom bunkers. The ones that aren't included in the disarmament treaties. They're part of a contingency program from 1981. We didn't trust the Russians to play fair with us. So we hid a dozen missile silos around the country. Nobody knows they're underground, nobody knows where to find them. The idea was, if the Russians did strike first, these silos would be off the maps, and unaffected by the initial nuclear exchange. Then, after the Russians had exhausted their armory, our crews would fire, and remove Moscow and other strategic targets from the board. The United States would win."

Zach laughed. "Win? Win what? A glow-in-the-dark wasteland? Everybody would be dead."

"Cade, if Barrows interrupts again, I want you to slap him. Nothing incapacitating. Just enough to shut him up."

"Yes sir," Cade said, with a flicker of a glance at Zach.

Zach shut up. That was a lawful order. He didn't want to be on the receiving end of any punishment Cade dished out. It would be too humiliating for both of them.

Wyman nodded, apparently satisfied.

"Yesterday, the crew missed its regular check-in," he said. "That means two things happen. First, we send an emergency response team to investigate. That's standard procedure. A squad from SEAL Team Gold went to Parker immediately to assess the situation."

Wyman hesitated.

Zach raised his hand. Wyman nodded, allowing him to speak.

"What happened?"

"They haven't responded since they arrived. That was eight hours ago. We re-tasked a satellite to look at Parker. No sign of the soldiers. Nothing out of the ordinary at all. It's like the town just swallowed them up."

"Has anyone tried contacting the authorities in Parker?" Zach asked. "I mean, they've got a police department, right?"

"I told you, this is a covert operation, Barrows," Wyman said. "As far as the locals know, the silo doesn't exist."

"So you called in the SEALs before you called the local cops."

Wyman shrugged. "Standard operating procedure."

"What is the second thing?" Cade asked.

Wyman hesitated again.

"You said two things happened when the missile crew failed to check in. What's the second?" Cade asked.

Wyman went a little gray under his orange makeup. Then he cleared his throat and looked down at the table.

"The second thing," he said. "The second thing that happens is that, after 24 hours without the entry of the all-clear codes, the computer at the silo will assume the crew has been killed and Washington D.C. has been compromised. It will then automatically launch the missile at its target."

"What?" Zach said.

Cade slapped him. Not hard, but it still stung like hell.

"Oh for God's sake. Cade, let him talk," Wyman said, annoyed.

"Ow," Zach said, rubbing his cheek. "What did you just say? You said that the missile will launch on its own?"

Wyman shrugged. "They tell me it's a fail-safe strategy, like our submarine crews. Just in case of total thermonuclear war, and the chain of command is severed."

"Why are these silos still active?" Zach said. "I don't know if you heard, but the Berlin Wall went down in 1989."

Wyman glared at him. "You think the missiles

went away just because the Soviet Union changed its name? You think those nukes in the Ukraine aren't still pointed right at us?"

"And this is your brilliant solution? Blow up the world even more?"

"This program existed long before I got here, Barrows," Wyman said. "Your hero Sam Curtis kept it going, just like every president before him. So spare me your indignation. We've got a little more than eight hours until nuclear war becomes a reality. Let's move it back into the hypothetical realm before we waste any more time debating. We have a jet waiting to take you to Wyoming. We can shave a little time and have you there in about two hours. From there, you can access the silo and take it offline. I've got a guy who will give you the codes."

"Yeah, but why me?" Zach said. "You could send Cade alone. Or you could find him another partner."

Wyman looked at Cade for a moment, then back at Zach. "He's had other partners. Believe it or not, you were the only one who managed to survive as long as you did. I figure maybe you're his lucky rabbit's foot, or maybe he just works better with you around."

Zach looked at Cade. "How many other partners have you been through?"

Wyman snapped before Cade could respond. "It doesn't matter. So. You going to answer the call of duty now? Or do you want to see how fast you can dig a bomb shelter?"

Zach shook his head. Like he would turn this down. If there were anything he could possibly do to help, of course he'd do it. Those were the stakes on the line.

But he was still curious about one thing.

"Why *us*, though?" Zach asked. "Why not send more soldiers?"

"Because we are looking at some unknown enemy that is near a secret installation of vital interest to national security, and can dispose of an entire squad of heavily armed, highly trained soldiers without leaving a trace. So, naturally, Cade, I thought of you."

Cade looked at Wyman blankly. Waiting for a direct order or question.

Wyman sighed. "Is there anything out there that we should know about in the Parker area? Anything that operates on" — he struggled for the right phrase — "your side of the line, so to speak?"

"Parker is not a known site of unusual events," Cade said. "This is most likely a human agency at work. Sir."

"Then you don't need either of us," Zach said. "Come on, Lester. This is stupid, even for you."

Wyman turned red under his layer of self-tanner. "Cade, I want you to slap Barrows every time he does not address me by my proper title."

Zach sighed and rolled his eyes. He had no desire to be slapped by Cade again — it really did sting — so he said, "Fine. Mr. President. This is stupid, even for you."

Wyman's eyes narrowed and he hunched in his chair like a toddler being told to eat his vegetables. "Oh, because you're so smart," he said. "As if you had any idea of the pressure I'm under every day."

God, Zach thought. He sits in the Oval Office.

Commands the most powerful military in human history. Has the attention of the entire world. And it's not enough to prop up that fragile ego.

"So tell me, Barrows, what would you do?" Wyman demanded.

"I would get the Joint Chiefs involved! I would send a full battalion of soldiers! I'd get everyone in the NSA figuring out a way to hack the silo remotely! I'd start talking to the Russians right now, so they know we're not actually planning a sneak attack!"

Wyman frowned as if all of this had genuinely never occurred to him. He thought for a moment. Then he said, "No."

"What?"

"I'm having enough troubles with the Russians on another thing. And if this got out in public, I could forget winning in November. No. We keep this in-house. Small. Surgical strike. You and Cade. You handle it. That's my decision."

He smiled, as if proud of himself.

Zach wanted to choke Wyman, but knew that would mean a swift and fatal response from Cade.

"Are you kidding me? You'd seriously risk nuclear war just to protect your chances in the next election?"

Wyman looked at him blankly, as if not comprehending the language Zach was speaking.

Zach rubbed his eyes. "Fine. We'll go. But don't blame me if it really is the end of the world."

CHAPTER SEVEN

PARKER, WYOMING.

DESPITE EVERYTHING, ZACH THOUGHT, THEY had plenty of time.

The silo was due to arm and launch its missile — a Minuteman III carrying a 475-kiloton W87 warhead, enough to punch the heart out of a good-sized city — promptly at 0600 hours, or six in the morning, if the proper fail-safe codes were not entered on schedule. Wyman was fuzzy on the details — of course — but he was pretty sure this missile was aimed directly at the Kremlin in Moscow.

If it launched, the Russian's air defenses would detect it almost immediately. There was a chance the missile could be intercepted or shot down, but it would already be too late. The Russians would launch their own counterstrike, and then everyone in the world would get to see if all those movies about living in a post-Apocalyptic landscape were accurate.

If there was anyone left to find out.

It was already past midnight in Wyoming by the time they got to Andrews, and Cade and Zach still had to travel 1,500 miles to get to the silo. So they were both loaded into the rear seats of a couple of F-15s and flown across the country at just over Mach 1.

Even at that speed, the van they'd borrowed from the air force base did not pull up outside the town limits of Parker until almost 4:30 a.m. MST.

Zach still wasn't too worried. If it was true that this was only a human threat, then he had nothing to worry about. They had almost two-and-a-half hours until the deadline, and the sun wouldn't rise until an hour after that. He'd seen Cade tear through an entire squad of heavily armed soldiers in a little under thirty seconds. Maybe there were people hiding in Parker capable of putting down a SEAL team, but they'd be worse than helpless against Cade.

So yeah. They had plenty of time.

Unless.

Unless Wyman was wrong, or lying.

Knowing Wyman as he did, Zach figured it was probably both.

In which case, they would need every second.

Cade put the van in park in the middle of the highway where it rose on a slight hill over the small town. He and Zach got out and looked down. Parker sat on a flat plain just below them, the streets and buildings laid out in a random sprawl.

It was completely dark. Not a single building had a light on. Not a single window glowed in the night.

"Well, that's not ominous at all."

Cade didn't reply. He'd been unusually silent — even for him — for the entire drive from the airfield since they'd landed.

Zach figured that had something to do with the fact that he was no longer wearing his cross. But he also figured that Cade would say something about it when he was ready.

Cade spoke.

"Stay here," he said.

Not exactly the confession Zach was expecting.

"What?"

"We have less than two hours before a global thermonuclear war," Cade said. "I don't have time to look after you and breach the silo. Stay here."

"You think I came all this way to sit in the van?"

"You do not need to come any further. Wyman didn't order that. There's clearly nothing for you to do here. Stay with the van. I can take care of this myself. I will come back when it's over."

"Hey. You don't know what's down there. And neither do I. You might need some help."

Cade turned and looked at him. "Do you imagine you could help me?"

"I've done it before."

"When?" Cade asked. There wasn't a trace of sarcasm in his voice.

"When? Are you serious? When we went up against Konrad, when we tracked down that guy in Mexico, when we stopped the guys who exploded, when we fought the lizard-things — "

"I recall you being taken hostage. Captured. Threatened. Almost killed. I recall having to deviate from my mission each time to rescue you. I am fairly sure I can do without that kind of help."

Zach looked at Cade, stunned into silence for a moment.

Cade was not human. He knew that. He *knew* that.

Even so, they had found a way to talk to one another. They'd made jokes, as well as Cade was able.

This was different. Then, Zach heard some echoes of humanity in Cade's voice. They'd treated one another as — well, not exactly equals. But as if they were on the same side.

As if they were friends.

Now Cade regarded Zach with the same detachment as he did everyone else. Like he was looking at a cut of meat in a butcher's case.

"Are you serious?" Zach said.

Cade just tilted his head. Right. Stupid question.

"Cade, has Wyman done something to you? Is there something wrong with you now? You're just passively following his orders."

"He's the president, Zach. That is my duty."

"You know who Wyman is — you know *what* he is. You know he doesn't belong in the White House. He's ruining this country."

"My opinion of the president is irrelevant," Cade said. "We have had a productive working relationship."

"Are you shitting me right now?"

Cade finally looked annoyed. It was only there for a moment, but Zach knew the expression well. He'd finally managed to piss the vampire off. Just like old times.

"No. I am not," Cade snapped. "I have spent almost four years tracking and breaking the operations of the Shadow Company, Zach — something I was not able to do under President Curtis. I have crippled the Company and killed a large number of their operatives. That is an objective good, no matter what else President Wyman has done."

The Shadow Company: The dark twin of the United States' intelligence-gathering agencies — an above-top-secret organization that operated out of the glare of public oversight, funded by black budgets and secret accounts, answering only to its own agenda. Like one of those strange fish at the bottom of the ocean, it had mutated and changed in the dark, under hidden pressures. It made deals with the devil — sometimes literally. Cade and Zach had fought its operatives before, and each time it cost too many innocent lives. Zach had no idea what the Shadow Company's ultimate goal was, but he had no doubt that it was evil.

"Well, that's super," Zach said. "But who gave you all that information on the Shadow Company? It was Wyman, right? Because he was working with them before. He was their inside man!"

"If that were true, that would be treason."

"Jesus Christ, will you stop talking like a robot! Of course it would be treason! You and I both know that! This is what we both talked about!"

"I had no proof then, and I have no proof now. Do you?"

Zach crossed his arms and looked away. He'd been in an office in Nebraska for four years. And even if he hadn't been, he would have had no idea where to start looking for evidence that Wyman was allied with the Shadow Company. "No," he admitted.

"Then he is still the president," Cade said, "and I follow his orders. Unless you have anything else to say, this is a waste of time. I need to reach the silo."

Zach realized something. He'd taken the name of the Lord in vain. And Cade had not scolded him. At least a couple of times in Cade's presence, and Cade hadn't said a word. That used to be the one thing you couldn't do around him.

And Cade was no longer wearing his cross.

"Cade," Zach said. "What happened to you?"

Cade hesitated. For a fraction of a second, an unusual flicker of emotion crossed his face. Something like... regret.

But then it was gone.

"I am able to do my job," he said. "That's all that matters."

He turned to leave.

"Stay here," he warned Zach. "Whatever is down there killed six highly trained soldiers. I'm sure you would not last as long as they did."

Then he was gone, faster than Zach's eyes could follow. All he felt was the breeze kicked up by Cade's passing.

Zach stood there, alone in the dark.

Just like old times.

CHAPTER EIGHT

C ADE MOVED.

His ears and eyes and nose all opened to the night around him as he ran.

Cade's senses were inhumanly sharp, capable of detecting a single drop of blood from a kilometer away, capable of marking the scent of a person in a room an hour or a month after they'd walked through it, capable of detecting an errant heartbeat from thirty feet. Cade could hear the telltale skip in a person's pulse that signaled they were anxious, or frightened, or lying.

President Wyman's heart had been pounding when he ordered them here, but it had been difficult to separate that from the man's usual anxiety, insomnia, and drug use. The president was taking a number of stimulants every day to keep himself awake and functioning, followed by heavy doses of tranquilizers to ward off his regular panic attacks. His heart was under constant strain, and Cade wondered sometimes how much more it could endure.

But even if Cade couldn't hear the lie in Wyman's

heartbeat, he picked it up the second they reached the outskirts of Parker.

He could smell it.

The entire place smelled wrong.

There was an odor, of something pungent and earthy and rotten, the scent of something left out too long in the sun, organic processes churning and growing on a deep, unseen level.

It was not quite like vegetation and not quite like spoiled meat. It was both, and neither.

And it was coming from all around the little town.

Wyman knew something about this place. More than he told them. That was nothing unusual. Better men than him had kept secrets from Cade.

But he'd sent them right into an ambush, as unprepared as the Navy SEALs before. Cade could handle that. Zach could not. Wyman clearly did not intend for Zach to come back from this mission.

So Cade would do what he could to keep Zach alive while still following orders. He would do this alone.

Cade would face whatever was growing here on his own. It would have to be enough.

If it wasn't, then Zach wouldn't be the only one to die.

He veered away from the town center, and headed toward the missile silo's hidden entrance.

It was beyond a chain-link fence at the outskirts of town — a flat, featureless cement rectangle, with a corrugated-steel shed at one side. A tall UHF/VF antenna, disguised as a metal windmill, loomed over the shed. It was meant to look like a ground-water pumping station, and it might have fooled anyone who didn't notice the long scam running down the middle of the cement.

Cade vaulted the seven-foot fence, practically flying over it, without breaking stride.

He came to a sudden, dead stop at the pump shed. If anyone had been watching, it would have seemed he just appeared out of thin air.

The metal sides of the shed were rusted in spots, and its door, closed by a weathered old padlock, looked as if it hadn't been opened in years.

But someone else had been here. Recently. Cade could smell that, too. Something had disturbed the air here. It wore the skin of a human being, but underneath, it was something... *other*. Something Cade had never encountered before.

That made him pause, but only for a second. The fact that this was something new — something unknown — was troubling. If he'd never faced it before, it was entirely possible that he was about to deal with a creature or entity that was stronger than he was.

He felt microwaves from a long-range scanner land on his skin like a light rain; the silo's security system had detected him. If there was anyone — or anything — down in the silo, they would know he was here.

But it didn't change anything. He still had to go through the door.

In his long afterlife, he had come across many inhuman things. Most of them were stronger than he was. So far, he'd managed to kill them all.

He reached out, snapped the padlock, and entered the shed.

Cade checked his watch, a high-tech timepiece

automatically synched via GPS with sunrise in every time zone he visited. A gift from a sometime friend.

One hour, nineteen minutes to go before launch.

CHAPTER NINE

ZACH SAT IN THE FRONT seat of the van, running the engine to keep the heater going. It was cold in Wyoming. Cade might not feel the weather, but Zach did.

He'd pulled the van to the side of the road, but he wasn't too worried about anyone driving up behind him. The highway was deserted. There was nothing in any direction except the dry, empty plains dotted with scrub brush. It was possible to feel like the last man on earth out here.

Then Zach saw something move.

Down on the town's main street, just at the edge of his vision. Something emerged from the shadows at the base of one of the buildings.

A street light flared back to life at that moment, revealing a man in dark camo fatigues walking across the asphalt.

It was one of the SEALs, or it was one of the locals who liked wearing hunting gear in the middle of the night.

Either way, Zach figured he should talk to the guy.

Cade might think he was helpless, or stupid, but he'd been through worse than this and survived. And he wanted some answers.

He put the van into drive and tapped on the gas, and slowly made his way down into Parker.

One hour, fourteen minutes to go.

CHAPTER TEN

CADE DESCENDED A METAL SPIRAL stair-case which went down a concrete shaft behind the facade of the pump shed. It ended on a small landing in front of a circular metal hatch that resembled a bank vault door.

The hatch had no handle, no outer hinges, and appeared to sit flush with the cement floor. There was only a keypad set into the surface. Cade entered the combination he'd been given. It didn't work. The keypad didn't respond at all.

There was either no power going to the hatch — which was unlikely since the entire silo complex ran on its own generators — or the combination had been changed to keep people out.

Cade entered another combination. No response. Then another. Still nothing.

He could keep entering combinations at random. Over time, he might hit upon the right one. By then the missiles would have launched and the sun would likely look down on the charred husk of the planet.

By now, alarms should have been sounding in the underground complex below. Cade knew he was visible to at least three security cameras. Heavily armed men should have been alerted to his presence.

But he heard nothing. No one was coming for him, guns blazing. They would have to open the hatch to do that.

Whoever was inside, they were content to wait Cade out.

So Cade went for the next option.

He dug his fingers into the reinforced concrete on either side of the hatch. It was softer than the steel, but not by much.

His skin peeled away from his muscle and bone, but he didn't stop.

Like a gardener pulling a weed, he searched with his fingers for some edge, some place to grip. He got the barest fingerhold on the rim of the hatch, a good six inches below.

Cade pulled, lifting from his knees.

For a long moment, nothing happened.

Then Cade heard something creak.

Metal began to rend, to deform, then to scream in protest.

If Cade hadn't been on a strict diet of healthy young red-blooded soldiers and terrorists lately, he doubted he would have the strength for this.

But he was capable of so much more these days.

He pulled harder, and with a sudden crack and shriek, the hatch came free as the bolts holding it in place sheared cleanly at their welds. Concrete vaporized under the pressure, and Cade stood in the cloud of gray dust, waiting to see if anything would leap out at him.

Again, nothing.

All that was there was another ladder, leading down. Emergency lights cast a weak glow into the darkness.

Cade tossed the hatch, which he'd been holding like a shield, to one side.

He dropped down into the hole.

Zach parked the van on the wrong side of the street, closest to the spot where the man in camouflage had vanished into the shadows between two buildings. One was a small supermarket and general store. The other was a Laundromat. Zach tried to imagine living here, in Parker, and washing his clothes in a small building with six or seven other people. Tried to imagine drinking at the bar at the end of the street and watching the game with the same six or seven people. Every single Sunday night for the rest of his life.

Now that was a horror movie.

He got out of the van, but left it running, with the door open. Despite all that time behind a desk, he hadn't forgotten everything he'd learned while working with Cade, and one of the most important lessons was: always have an exit route.

Zach tapped his phone into flashlight mode. He swept the beam of the light across the small alley.

The ground was covered in gravel, and there were garbage cans by a side door to the Laundromat. But other than that, nothing.

Zach checked his phone. Zero bars. Big surprise. He'd been given a satphone for emergency calls back to the White House, but it was large and bulky and he'd left it in the van. Once upon a time, he'd had a cool piece of spy-tech for a phone, which could call out from underground prison sites, decrypt coded messages, block electronic eavesdropping, and act as a homing signal for Cade. But Wyman had taken that, along with his old job. Now he had his iPhone.

Zach looked up from the screen and nearly jumped out of his skin.

The man in camo was standing there, right in front of him, hands in his pockets.

And he was smiling.

CHAPTER ELEVEN

CADE DESCENDED THE LADDER AND found a small foyer with an elevator. There was another keypad, but he didn't bother with it this time. Instead, he pulled open the blast-hardened doors, revealing the shaft.

It was a hydraulic system, so there was no cable lifting the elevator up and down. It ran on wheels that rolled in tracks set into the side walls of the shaft.

He looked down. A dozen yards below, the elevator was stuck in place, blocking the shaft like a stone lodged in someone's throat.

Cade stepped into the empty air and landed on the elevator with a heavy thud.

As he'd learned once before, even secret military installations had to follow OSHA codes. There was an access panel in the elevator ceiling in case anyone got stuck inside. He lifted it open and dropped inside.

He pulled open the doors and saw bare concrete.

The elevator had been stopped in the middle of the shaft. Cade couldn't get out.

Fine, he thought. We'll do this the hard way.

He leaped up through the access panel again and found the elevator's brakes. All four were locked in place, freezing the wheels in the tracks.

Cade reached over and pulled the first brake free from the wheel in the track. The elevator didn't move. He did the next. The elevator lurched slightly with a hissing noise. He snapped the third, and the hiss grew louder, like an angry serpent. He was ready when he pulled the fourth and last brake, and the elevator suddenly sank away under his feet.

He fell after it.

It picked up a surprising amount of speed in such a short distance. It sounded like a plane crash when it hit, the noise echoing on the concrete, a wave of pressurized air shooting back up the shaft.

Cade landed on his feet on the crumpled metal roof of the elevator car. Dust flew everywhere. He was temporarily deafened by the noise, standing in a pool of silence.

He went through the access panel again. The elevator's hard landing had blown open the external doors of the elevator.

He was in the real heart of the silo now.

He stepped forward, into the dark.

Cade entered the corridor leading to the Launch Control Center. The corridor was a tube that reached from the elevator and the entry shaft to the area where the two-person missile crew lived and worked for months at a time. It extended forward twenty feet before ending in another hatch, which was closed and sealed with a wheeled door to maintain the air pressure. It was like standing in a submarine buried in the dirt.

Cade put one foot down on the grating that served as a floor in the tube.

As if triggered by his weight, the hatch at the other end of the tube opened, and a man walked out. He wore a military uniform in the gray-grid pattern of night-camouflage. One of the SEAL team.

Then Cade caught a whiff of him. No. Not a man. Not anymore.

It still held a man's shape. Still wore a man's skin. But it had been filled with something else. Whoever had been in that body before, he was long dead. Now something else walked around in his boots.

"Step aside," Cade told it. Maybe it still spoke English.

The thing inside the SEAL's skin opened its mouth, and a strangely musical voice replied.

"We know what you are," it said. The SEAL was not breathing. It moved his chest only to speak to Cade, to push air through vocal cords like a musician playing an instrument. It sounded almost like a flute vibrating underwater.

"Then you know you should step aside," Cade said. "You can't stop me."

It smiled hugely at him, the skin on the SEAL's face peeling back away from dry white teeth.

Behind it, the hatch opened again. Five more dead SEALs stepped through into the tight corridor. They formed a wall.

Cade smelled the same corruption, whatever it was, on each of them. The men who'd been sent here, now all dead and turned into conscripts for the Other Side.

Cade would try to end their service as quickly as possible.

He began walking along the metal grating toward the dead SEALs.

They marched forward to meet him, in a single-file line, all with that same too-wide grin. They didn't carry any weapons. Perhaps they didn't think they'd need them.

"All right then," Cade said. "Let's begin."

He blurred into motion then, and flew across the gap and hit the first corpse like a hammer swung by an angry god.

One hour, twelve minutes to go.

CHAPTER TWELVE

ZACH SWORE AND JUMPED BACK. The man in camo had not been there a second before. He had not been behind the garbage cans. There was no way Zach could have missed him

And yet, there he was. He kept grinning at Zach. Zach could see now that this was not one of the SEALs. He was just a guy, in his late 40s, bundled up in hunting gear against the cold. If Zach had been running prep for this mission, he would have had a photo ID for everyone in town, based off the state's DMV database. But because Wyman's people were running it, he and Cade had been sent in with a road map and not much else.

"Hey," Zach said. "I didn't see you there. I'm Zach."

The man grinned. Said nothing.

Zach tried again. "You all right? I'm with the federal government. We're here to help."

"I know," the man said. His voice was strange, like someone who'd been sucking helium. Zach took an instinctive step back. He wondered if his inoculations against zombie infection were still good.

"Right," Zach said. "You know. Great. Can you tell me what's going on here? What's your name?"

"We don't have any names," the man said, his voice trilling weirdly. "But you will see what is happening here. Very soon."

And I am done with this bullshit, thank you very much, Zach thought, and stepped back again. When the locals start talking like that, it's time to jump out and nuke the whole site from orbit.

"Super," Zach said, keeping his eyes on the man while he walked backwards. "I'm just going to get my phone and make a call, okay? We can tell everyone about it — "

Zach was back out into the street. He planned to get into the van and get as far away from here as possible. He turned around to jump inside —

And realized he couldn't.

Something had a hold on his leg. He looked down, and saw that the gravel of the alley had risen to swallow his foot. Something was pulling on him now. Hard.

Zach kicked at it with his free foot, and realized there was something wrong with it. It didn't crunch. It wasn't gravel at all. It was some kind of moss or something. It only looked like little individual pebbles. Up close, he could see it was more like a carpet, covering the ground.

Zach pulled harder and it tore. His shoe popped free, and he fell on his ass.

He looked up, and saw the man in camo walking slowly toward him.

His feet were covered, ankle-deep, by the weird carpeting. He didn't walk so much as wade through the stuff all over the ground as he moved toward Zach.

And he was still smiling.

CHAPTER THIRTEEN

CADE SHOULD HAVE BEEN WINNING.
He hit the dead SEALs over and over. He threw them against the metal walls of the tube hard enough to shatter every bone in their bodies. He'd broken and twisted their spines, and caved in their skulls.

They just kept getting up. Every time he crushed or crippled one, another got back up and stood in his way.

Cade grabbed the dead SEAL in front of him and flung him against the ceiling. It sounded like a pillow hitting a bed. Anything solid in the man's body was long gone. And yet, it kept moving, kept rebounding, a boneless tube of solid muscle and fiber.

Cade threw the SEAL away over his shoulder, putting it behind him, only to face the next dead SEAL in line. Its skin was mottled now, gray and beaten like old canvas, but not broken or bleeding. It still had that same grin on its face.

Cade so badly wanted to wipe that grin away.

He punched the SEAL in the face. It was like

hitting a haystack. The impact went right through it. The head snapped back on its neck and the grin was back again.

Cade felt the arms of the other dead SEAL grab him from behind. Another one came around and grabbed his wrist. He was smothered by their bodies.

All jammed in the narrow space together, there was no place for him to run or dodge. He'd been hit harder than this before. But it was starting to add up.

He had not gotten further than the middle of the corridor. They were like a sponge stuffed in the tube, taking the worst he could give and simply absorbing it.

He didn't know how long he'd been at this. They were frustratingly resilient. They didn't make a sound, no matter what he did.

He'd fought dead men before. Zombies, vampires, Frankensoldiers. Their bodies — like his own — had been changed, made tougher, upgraded by a biological shift that turned them into something different, but still obeyed the basic rules of their human forms. They still worked like skeletons wrapped in muscle.

These things didn't. They had a human form, but they were something entirely different inside.

They were separate bodies but fought like a swarm. Humans could be relied upon to trip up one another, to get in one another's way. Even the most finely trained military units were individuals, using individual thought and action. They could predict where their fellow soldiers would move next, but occasionally, they would be wrong.

These five bodies were always perfectly coordinated. As soon as one stepped up and was knocked down, the others knew where to hit Cade, where to press their attack, where to retreat. Dodging one push him into the blow of another.

Cade finally realized what he'd been doing wrong. He'd been fighting them like men.

He had to treat them as a single cell, and cripple the entire organism.

Quickest way to do that: massive, irreparable damage.

He started biting.

His fangs extended, and he snapped forward with the motion that was so much like a tiger severing the neck and spine of its prey. He got a good chunk of the throat of the closest soldier, and felt the old thirst in him rise, his mouth filling with saliva as he anticipated the warm, salty rush of blood.

He gagged as something dry and powdery filled his mouth instead.

Cade felt something solid in his mouth, shoving past his teeth, pushing back. It tasted of dry earth and dead leaves. It smelled of closed-off spaces, long-sealed coffins, cellars and basements and the undersides of boxes buried for years in the dirt.

He staggered backward, surprised that he still had the capacity for horror, felt it trying to push its way down his esophagus. He sealed off his throat, and in his shock, managed to shake off all of the dead SEALS.

But the thing was covering his face now, trying to get in through his nostrils, crawling over his eyes, toward his ears.

He stepped back again, used both hands like

claws and scraped it off. He spat fiercely, ejecting all traces of it from his mouth. He flung the fragments as far away as he could, heard them splat against the metal of the tube.

Able to see again, he noticed the SEALS waiting for him. The one in the lead had a large hole where his neck met his shoulder. It was filled with yellowish fiber. There was no blood. No fluid at all.

Before Cade could get a good look, the SEAL stepped forward, arm out, ready to grab Cade again.

Cade took a solid grip on the arm. The dead SEAL tried to slip away as they'd all done before, but Cade grabbed the SEAL's shoulder at the same time and pushed while he pulled.

The arm stretched to an impossible length.

Then, finally, the skin of the dead man ripped and gave way. It sounded like a tree stump coming free from hard earth.

For a moment, Cade simply stood and stared. The dead SEAL stared back.

Then it looked down at the open wound where its arm used to hang.

All that remained was a dry spot that dangled yellowish cords of some kind of fiber.

Cade looked down at the arm, still tight in his grip. It was already falling apart, crumbling into chunks that burst into dust as they hit the steel floor.

The yellowish cords fattened and grew before Cade's eyes, swelling like some kind of jungle vine growing fat after a heavy rainfall, branching out into a hand and fingers. After another second, the dead SEAL had a new arm, no longer mimicking the color of flesh, but the solid gray of an oak branch. Yet it flexed and moved as if it were made of rubber.

Cade had to admit it: this world was still capable of surprising him.

The smell of dry rot was everywhere now, all around him. Something fungal. Something terribly, terribly old.

Cade dropped the arm and it disintegrated completely. He spat again, still trying to get the taste out of his mouth.

"You can't stop me," he said to whatever was driving their bodies.

"We don't have to stop you," the first SEAL said, again in that strangely musical voice.

The same voice came from the open mouth of another SEAL. "We only have to slow you down."

Cade's watch beeped

Fifty-nine minutes, fifty-nine seconds to go.

CHAPTER FOURTEEN

ZACH STOOD UP, GRABBED HIS shoe, and ran as fast as he could for the van. He slammed the door shut and put his foot on the gas. The van's tires spun for a second before they gripped the asphalt, and then he was moving forward. Zach cranked the wheel and turned back toward the edge of the town.

He was scrabbling with one hand for the satphone on the passenger seat when the man in camo stepped in front of the van.

Zach swerved to miss him. But not far enough.

The man went down under the wheels. The van bounced like it was going over a speed bump. Zach felt, more than heard, the impact of the man's body.

Zach hit the brakes and the van skidded to a halt. He got out, and looked back in the street.

Zach was pretty sure the guy wasn't human. This wasn't his first day on the job, after all. But there was a chance that there was still someone worth saving back there. Zach had seen people twisted into monsters before. Maybe none of them had made it back yet, but that didn't mean none of them ever would.

So he walked, slowly and carefully, to the man's body.

It didn't move.

Zach stood over the lumpy shape in the street.

The man in camo was facedown. The van's tires had left big furrows in his back and legs. He wasn't breathing.

Zach sagged with the sudden weight of another death on his conscience, another civilian he hadn't been able to save. It had been a while since he'd felt this kind of guilt.

Then the man's head turned completely around to look at Zach, and it was still grinning.

Zach screamed, leaped back, and pulled the Smith & Wesson Governor from his coat pocket and fired two shots at the man in the street.

Sure, he felt bad about hitting the guy, but he wasn't a complete idiot. Anything that can come up smiling after being run down by a van is not even remotely human anymore.

Zach had been carrying the gun ever since he'd left Nebraska. The Secret Service had not even searched him for it.

The .45s punched right into the man's chest at point-blank range.

And he was still getting up.

He smiled at Zach, and his grin became even wider, until it split his face, until his head fell open as if on a hinge, and something emerged from the man's mouth like an antenna extending.

Zach wondered for a moment why he'd ever missed this job.

Then he started running.

CHAPTER FIFTEEN

CADE TRIED TO THINK AS the dead SEALs swarmed over him again. It wasn't easy. They just kept pounding at him.

Now he understood why they didn't carry any weapons. It was not because they were arrogant or overconfident. It wasn't about them at all. They didn't want Cade to take any weapons from them. They expected him to fight hand-to-hand. They really did know him.

He would have to figure out how that was possible. Once he finished killing these things.

Hand-to-hand, his options were badly limited. They were able to absorb whatever punishment he could give. He couldn't bruise or break them. There was nothing in the tube to use as a weapon. The metal grating and the steel plates on the walls were all too solidly riveted into place, and he doubted they would give him a chance to pry anything free.

It was fairly obvious he couldn't win this fight. Not like this.

So Cade curled into a ball on the floor.

They dogpiled on top of him and began beating

him with everything they had. Cade took it.

He didn't want them to see what he was doing.

This was going to hurt, but that was all right. Cade needed a weapon, and he could take the pain.

As their fists and boots rained down on him, Cade used his thumbnail to slice open his left forearm. He peeled back the skin and muscle, laying the arm open to the bone. There was little blood, which was no surprise. Cade's body hung onto every drop.

Although Cade had ceased to be human a long time before, his basic skeletal anatomy was more or less the same. His internal organs had shifted and changed, his skin and muscle was much denser than ever before, but he was still put together in pretty much the same way as a regular person. Knee bones connected to shin bones, hip bones to thigh bones, and so on. Fibula, tibia, vertebrae, sternum, clavicle.

And in his forearm, radius and ulna.

Cade decided he could function with only one of those for a while.

He snapped the ulna, the bone in his forearm on the side that led to his little finger. He wanted to keep the use of his thumb, if at all possible. And with a swift jerk, he yanked the bone free of his tendons and cleanly out of his arm with a short sucking noise.

Then he began to rub the narrow end against the metal floor.

His bones were tough — a little stronger than cast iron, though much lighter. But the floor was tough enough to wear them down, especially at the speed he was rubbing.

All through this, the dead SEALS kept hitting him. He was getting very tired of it.

So when he sprang back to his feet, he used his own sharpened ulnar bone to stab the nearest one through the head.

That stopped it. It spasmed on the end of Cade's improvised bone knife, and struggled. Cade quickly withdrew the pointed bone and then slashed with the edge, slicing the dead SEAL's head clean off its body.

Again, there was no blood, only that yellowish fiber.

But this time, the entire body crumbled to powder.

The other SEALS swarmed Cade again, but they were not fast enough to pin his arm with the bone knife. He sliced and slashed through them, and they lost arms, fingers, and other chunks of their bodies.

They fell to pieces, collapsing into fragments on the metal floor.

In a moment, Cade stood alone in the tube, surrounded by the wreckage of their bodies and a lot of dust, his left arm hanging oddly at the elbow.

He checked his watch.

Forty-eight minutes to go.

CHAPTER SIXTEEN

A T THIS POINT IN HIS life, Zach was still surprised how his mind could turn to the strangest details even when he was pants-wettingly close to being horribly killed.

He should have been thinking about how he just witnessed a man's head split open like a clamshell and how best to make it back to the car without being eaten by the thing that oozed out of the wreckage. Instead, he was thinking about a college biology course, even as he ran as fast as he could.

Zach had already had plans for his future by the time he got to Dartmouth, so he was less interested in broadening his mind or new challenges than he was maintaining a perfect GPA for his resume. That's why he picked what was looked like an easy class for his biology credit: "The Fungus Among Us." He figured anything with a title like that had to be a gut course.

He was wrong. He found the class was taught by Dr. Eric Mansen, a man with a beard like a Biblical prophet and a passion for spores, molds, and fungus. He recited facts about the various members of the kingdom of *Fungi* like he was reeling off the names of saints, and expected his students to share his devotion, at least if they wanted an A. Zach probably should have dropped the class, but he missed the deadline, and ended up working harder than he ever thought possible memorizing facts about mushrooms and all their relatives.

It was, Zach had to admit, fascinating stuff. Fungi could survive for centuries, seemingly dormant, before springing back to life. Fungi were the dominant life form on earth for millions of years. They came out of the sea 1.3 billion years ago, long before any other species. They survived following the meteor impact that killed the dinosaurs, rising in great tree-like columns more than three stories high, thriving while other creatures died because they did not need light. And they fed off the dead and decaying.

Fungi could sit, undetected, under the dirt in a forest or field, before rising to claim whatever animals or plants happened to die on the ground.

"Fungi are sentient," Mansen had insisted in one lecture, eyes blazing, a large slide of a mature *Ophiocordyceps unilateralis* sprouting from a carpenter ant's body. "Any living thing walks across a forest floor, and the fungi know it. They send their mycelium up to the surface after their prey."

All of this was how Zach figured out what was chasing him: he'd seen it before on that slide in Mansen's classroom.

Cordyceps: a kind of parasitic fungus that infiltrates the bodies of living animals and makes its way straight to their brains. Once there, it forces them to find the most beneficial place for the fungus to reproduce. And then, the animal waits, until the fungus finally erupts, bursting from its body and releasing spores, infecting other hosts, and repeating the process over and over again.

Something very much like that was sprouting from what used to be the man in camo's head.

So Zach figured if he didn't want the same thing to happen to him, he'd better run.

He was halfway back to the van when the spore-headed man landed in front of him, cutting off his escape. It had leaped over his head, landed as lightly as a cat — or Cade — in front of him.

It couldn't see Zach — its eyes had peeled away with the rest of its skull — but its arms were out, grasping for him, trying to pull him into an embrace.

Zach knew if that thing caught him, he'd be turned into a vessel for whatever was rooted inside it, made into a host just the same way.

He already knew the .45 ammunition wouldn't stop it. He reached into his heavy jacket and came out with a different set of shells and jammed them into the Governor. The spore-headed body lunged for him and missed.

Zach sidestepped, raised the gun, and fired.

The first blast went a little wide, but that was all right. It wasn't as if sniper-like accuracy was required at this distance. The shells he'd loaded were custom-made. They were called Dragon's Breath by the manufacturer. They were loaded with magnesium pellets that exploded upon firing, launching a 4,000-degree sheet of flame at anything within thirty feet of the barrel.

Zach had done this too many times in his life

already. As Cade had pointed out, he'd already been captured and tortured and terrorized by any number of living, breathing nightmares. So he'd decided a while ago to have more options than just fleeing for his life when something tried to eat him. He'd found that while many monsters were bulletproof, almost all of them were flammable.

The spore-headed man went up like dry kindling.

It wandered around a few more flaming steps before it fell to the ground. The gray carpet on the street retreated from the smoldering remains of its body.

Zach emptied the magnesium shell and shook his hand quickly. The gun got extraordinarily hot when he fired those rounds. He'd be lucky to get four more shots before it jammed or fouled.

Which was a real problem, because the doors of several buildings on the street opened just then.

And a dozen of the residents of Parker, Wyoming, walked out and began moving in Zach's direction. All of them smiling as if they were insanely happy to see him.

CHAPTER SEVENTEEN

THERE WAS NO RESISTANCE AS Cade spun the handle on the hatch at the end of the corridor. It swung open easily.

Cade left it open behind him as he stepped through.

The silo's control center was small and cramped, never meant to hold more than a few people at any one time. Every square inch of space was expensive, so, like a space capsule or a European bathroom, everything was designed for maximum efficiency.

But the equipment here was all like something out of a museum of the 20th century. Computer monitors with tiny green cathode-ray tubes were set into the walls. Banks of equipment were marked with the names of dead brands and long-bankrupt government contractors. Here and there, an obsolete piece of technology was replaced with a modern upgrade, a hard drive the size of a deck of cards hanging from wires in an empty space big enough to hold a refrigerator. This silo had been running off the books since the Cold War, with the kind of jerry-rigged repairs Cade had seen before in black-budget sites. Government bureaucracies always required receipts and authorization, which was a problem for places that weren't supposed to exist. So the people running the sites often made do with whatever they could find or scrape together on their own.

But now it was all covered with a phantasmagoric variety of colors and textures as weird things grew and sprouted on every surface, in every corner. The walls were thick with violently purple fur that seemed to ripple as if breathing. The floors had a garden of bright yellow slime molds clustered to the walls. Mushrooms popped up in the full spectrum of the rainbow. Hundreds of them covered the center of the tiny space, a little forest dotting the lumps that used to be the two airmen who sat in the chairs in front of the Missile Launch System.

The airmen were just barely visible. Their bodies were completely engulfed, and only their heads appeared above the piles of fungus that had colonized them. Mushrooms burst from their ears, clustered around their noses and mouths, rooted themselves in their scalps and entwined their stalks through their hair.

Only their eyes were still open as they stared blankly at the countdown to launch on their screens.

Forty-seven minutes to go.

CHAPTER EIGHTEEN

ZACH HURRIED TOWARD THE VAN and hopped into the front seat and jammed the shifter into drive. There was absolutely no reason to stick around here. He wanted to get as far away from the lurching citizens of Parker as possible. Then he'd use the satphone and call for reinforcements. He and Cade needed to sterilize this place.

He was halfway down the street when the asphalt in front of him buckled and the ground split open.

It looked like the roots of a massive tree suddenly shot up into the air, blocking the road. They reached toward the van, a tangled mass of organic matter, grasping and clawing for the windshield.

Zach turned the wheel as hard to the left as he could manage.

The tires skidded and bit, then lost their grip as the vehicle fishtailed around. Zach felt himself leave the seat as the van started to tip, and then toppled over completely, coming down hard on its side.

The van came to a shuddering halt. There was safety glass all over the interior of the cabin. Zach had lost a second, probably when his head hit the ceiling. He struggled with the airbag, shoved it out of his way, then looked out the cracked windshield.

The dozen or so people looked almost normal as they walked toward him, their feet moving easily through the gray stuff on the ground. There was a local cop in his uniform, an old man in a flannel shirt, a grandmotherly looking woman with styled gray hair and an actual goddamn apron, as if she'd just come from a church bake sale.

They were in no great hurry to get to him. They almost looked serene as they glided over the ground.

Zach searched quickly for the satphone. Found it on the ceiling near his head. Felt a sharp twinge in his shoulder as he snagged it — he'd landed badly on it — then kicked open the driver's side door and rolled out.

He still had his gun in one pocket, but it wouldn't kill all of the things walking toward him.

He heard the sound of tortured metal crumpling, and saw the long, root-like structures close around the van like a fist, crushing it as they drew tighter.

Zach looked down. Something was burrowing under the asphalt, heading for him. He needed a spot to make a stand, and make a call.

He ran for the bar, on his right.

Maybe it was because his father had been a drunk, but he'd always felt safe in bars. Zach had a lot of childhood memories set in dark, cool spaces lined with bottles.

He sprinted through the door and slammed and locked it behind him. The air was warm and thick inside, filled with the smell of rot and digestion.

Mildew covered everything, thick as fur on the walls, strung gossamer-thin like cobwebs from the ceiling.

Then he turned around and saw what had happened to the other residents of Parker.

They were laid out on the floor, their bodies piled on top of one another, decomposing into indistinguishable heaps. The people on the bottom of the pile were little more than bones overlaid with thick webs of fungus. But the people on the top — the more recent additions — were just beginning to break down. Their faces were still frozen in their wide grins.

Mulch. It had turned them all into mulch. So it could grow.

Zach gagged, then got it under control. He'd seen worse things.

Just not for a while.

Zach checked out the front window of the bar. The walking fungal hosts were gathered by the front door. They were not coming in — perhaps they didn't want to hurt the things still growing inside — but he couldn't get out that way.

He saw another exit in the back, with a skinny path between the piles of compost all over the floor.

He walked carefully and quickly through the heaps of mold, his shirt over his mouth and nose, trying not to breathe out of fear of infection and because of the smell in equal measure.

On the bar, in a patch barely touched by the fungal rot, was a thin plastic wrapper with a bright logo. On impulse, Zach grabbed it, hoping his gloves would keep it from spreading whatever this contagion was.

His right foot crushed something he couldn't see. As if in response, one of the bodies on the floor turned to him, the skin mostly gone from its skull, staring at Zach with blank eye sockets. Its mouth opened and began to split.

Zach used another magnesium shell on it, and it started to burn.

The other fruiting bodies began to stir as well. Tendrils snaked out of their shells, groping toward him.

Zach's path to the back door was suddenly blocked by all the writhing fungal life in the small space. He realized why the creatures outside didn't bother to chase him in here. They were already inside with him. He was fooled by their appearance. They weren't separate. They were all one creature. One thing that had already eaten the entire town and used it for a mask.

Zach thought fast. He saw that the bottles of liquor behind the bar were still mostly intact.

He fired a round into the booze, sending glass and fire blooming out in a brilliant burst of heat and light. A sheet of flame climbed up to the ceiling instantly and found a whole room full of fuel.

He could have sworn he heard something scream as the temperature skyrocketed and the fungus began to burn.

The tendrils retreated from the flames. Zach had a clear shot at the exit again. He ran out the rear door and hoped nothing was waiting for him on the other side.

CHAPTER NINETEEN

CADE DID NOT TOUCH THE two airmen. He knew they were beyond saving. He knew he was usually immune to any infection that might nest in a human being — the vampire part of him was essentially a parasitic organism itself, and it hated any competitors — but he'd never seen anything quite like this before. Not even in Innsmouth.

So he kept a careful distance.

He didn't know if the airmen's eyes were still working. They did not blink. He took a step closer.

Then the fungus all around him quivered in place on all the walls and surfaces around him, and air moved in the still chamber. The airmen's mouths opened, and the strange, flutelike voice spoke again.

"You cannot stop this," it said.

"I've heard that before," Cade said.

"The time for negotiation is past," the voice said. "We offered terms. We offered a compromise. Now we are at war. Your leader has sent you too late."

"I wasn't aware of any negotiations," Cade said.

Cade heard a whirring noise. A gigantic, antique reel-to-reel videotape drive spun to life on the wall.

One of the screens near Cade flickered to life. Cade saw static, and then he saw Wyman's face, looking greener than usual through the antique video feed.

"— here, I'm here," Wyman said in the recording.

The flutelike voice of the fungal mass responded to him. "We have attempted to communicate with you. We have sent messages."

Wyman kept glancing away from the camera. "What do you mean? Who are you? What do you want?"

"It has taken us this long to learn what you are. How to talk to you," the mass said. "We are using these parts of you to speak to these parts of us."

Cade realized it was some kind of colony creature — a sentient mass organism, its intelligence contained and distributed throughout all of its parts — and it assumed humanity was the same way. That the people it has absorbed were simply pieces of the whole.

"You have become malignant," the mass told Wyman. "You are threatening the whole. You are toxic. You must stop. Or we will use this place, this facility, to stop you."

Cade could see Wyman straighten up, a rooster fluffing its feathers to appear larger. "You cannot threaten the United States of America. You do not get to dictate terms to me."

"You must stop."

"Now listen here, whoever or whatever the hell you are, we have enough nukes to blow up the planet a dozen times over. You think you can scare me with just one? Think again."

"You are not threatening us," the voice said.

"You think I'm not threatening you? I will turn you into ash. Whoever you are — "

There was movement off screen, to the side of the camera on Wyman. Muttered words swallowed by the poor audio. Strident tones. "What? Who cares?" Wyman said. "Screw that, I won't — What?"

On the video, Wyman stood, moved out of the camera's eye. More muttering. Cade distinctly heard Wyman snap, "So we lose Wyoming. Big deal." Then Wyman returned, a moment later. "We do not negotiate with terrorists! So you better know who you're screwing with here, buddy. I will rain fire down on you and piss on the ashes —"

"No," the voice of the mass replied. "You will not."

The screen filled with static. The tape ended there.

Cade grimaced. Leave it to Wyman to speak to an alien species with only the barest understanding of human culture and yet still find a way to insult it.

He turned to the dead airmen, wrapped in the clinging veils of thick mold.

"What are you?" Cade asked.

"We are the future," it said. "You cannot stop us."

Then their bodies burst open, and Cade found himself wrapped in thick fungal ropes that twisted around his head, covering his eyes, pulling him off-balance, lashing him to the floor with extraordinary strength. The knife he'd fashioned from his own bone was knocked away, clattering to the floor somewhere out of reach. He pulled and clawed with both hands, but couldn't get a proper grip.

He the fungus crawl into him again. Felt tiny, needle-thin cilia extending upward through his nostrils and mouth, but not trying to choke him this time.

Now it was reaching for his brain.

CHAPTER TWENTY

THE ALLEY BEHIND THE BAR was deserted. Zach breathed a sigh of relief and ran fast, emptying the spent shells from the Governor as he moved. He felt the heat even through his gloves, and the cylinder wouldn't close properly. It was useless for the time being; it really wasn't meant to fire burning metal. If he still had access to the government's resources, he would have had someone build him something that could.

If he got out of this alive he'd look into that.

For now, he needed to find a place where the fungus couldn't follow.

That wasn't going to be easy. If there was one thing he learned from Mansen's class back in college, it was that fungus could survive anything, anywhere. There were varieties that thrived off heat, tolerated cold, could regrow after fires, loved water, happily ate toxic waste, even gobbled up radiation.

And just like that, Zach suddenly figured out what was happening here.

He had to make a call. Then he had to find Cade.

Zach ran down the alley until he found the back entrance to the Parker Laundromat. He kicked open the fire exit and went inside to the sound of an alarm ringing in his ears.

Fungi were tough, hardy and spread easily, but you could kill them. Fire worked. And so did chemicals.

Zach saw that there was mold and mildew all around the Laundromat, drawn by the water and the heat and the piles of stagnant clothes. But there was a wide open space, untouched by any of the dark strands of fungus. That's where the bleach and detergents sat on a shelf.

Zach grabbed a tiny, fist-sized bottle of Clorox and dumped it out all around him, like a magician would pour out a protective circle of salt. It worked. The black filaments on the floor shrank back as if stung. He dropped it, opened another, splashed it around. The fungus retreated.

Good. Maybe that would keep the creature — whatever it was — from finding him. Just to be safe, Zach splashed bleach over his shoes and feet, then his hands. Anything that might have touched the stuff.

Zach tossed the empty bottle of bleach, then took another and held it ready. He had cleared a tiny space. He took out the satphone and dialed a number dredged from memory. He hoped to God Wyman had been too lazy to change it.

Fortunately, someone picked up immediately. The government might be crumbling behind the scenes, but you could always rely on the bureaucracy to cover the phones. An aggressively bored male voice with a flat Midwestern accent answered.

"Authentication."

"This is Zachary Barrows, attached to CODE-NAME NIGHTMARE PET. I don't know the daily authentication. I'm on temporary assignment. My clearance is JACKAL CLERIC GREEN. Verification is SCREAMING BLUE MESSIAH."

The flat Midwestern voice suddenly sounded interested. And tense. "One moment. Verifying."

"Take your time, I've got nothing going on here…" Zach could see out the window of the Laundromat. The people in Parker had gathered out front. Still smiling at him.

A moment later, the voice came back on the line.

"You have provisional authentication, Mr. Barrows. Took a while to find you in our system. You've been out of the loop for a while, but I see you were recently reactivated. For your future reference, the daily authentication is — "

"I don't need it. What I need is an air strike on my GPS position. A MOAB. At least one. As soon as possible. Within the hour at the very latest."

A pause. A MOAB was technically known as the GBU-43, or the Massive Ordnance Air Bomb. Its real name was the Mother Of All Bombs, and it was the largest explosive device in the U.S. arsenal short of a nuclear weapon. It weighed almost 22,000 pounds and carried the destructive force of 11 tons of TNT.

"Is that all?" the voice on the line asked. Something about that Midwestern military accent. It was really good at understated sarcasm.

"No. I want you to follow that with a Hellfire missile strike. Immediately."

"Sir. You are sitting on top of a nuclear launch

facility — "

"I'm well aware of that. You level this place, burn it down to the bedrock. The missile won't fire if you destroy it in the silo. The warhead won't go off. Or if it does, well, at least it won't start World War III."

"But sir, that is going to leave nothing but a smoking crater where you are."

"Yeah," Zach said. "If we're lucky."

Another pause. Zach knew exactly how much weight his clearance carried. He once had the authority to order drone strikes and have satellites re-tasked, just on his say-so. Whoever was on the other end of the line didn't have the rank or the right to ask him why he wanted this. And he also knew he probably didn't want to know the reason, either.

"I'll have to get clearance from the president," he finally said.

Zach checked his watch. Thirty-eight minutes to go before launch.

"You do that. I'll hold."

CHAPTER TWENTY-ONE

CADE FELT IT TRYING TO take him over. Felt it worming inside his skull, speaking to him in a language that echoed inside his brain.

It had existed quietly, silently, for millennia before the first ancestor of humanity heaved itself out of the primordial sea. Cade watched as centuries passed. Dinosaurs walked the earth. Continents drifted. A small primate stood on its hind legs on the African savannah to escape the heat. Glaciers advanced and retreated.

It continued, unperturbed, a nation of many parts, sharing the same consciousness but separate bodies, hidden deep in the earth.

It survived multiple extinction events, watching other species exit the planet. It survived every one, living on geological time.

But now it was facing another extinction, and this time, it was worried. The entire planet was becoming toxic. The temperature was rising. The waters were becoming thick with chemicals that choked it, and plastics and metals it couldn't digest. It made a decision.

It decided to offer humanity one last chance. It took over Parker, infiltrating the bodies and minds of the residents with its spores, and then assumed control of the missile silo. It aimed a gun at humanity's head, and gave its demands.

It didn't like the answer.

So now it would launch a nuclear missile, and humanity would die. The colony would survive. It could absorb radiation. It didn't need sunlight to grow. And it would have plenty to eat during a nuclear winter. It could feed on the bodies of 7.5 billion people.

It tried to sound reasonable as it spoke to Cade, inside his mind. This is for the best, it seemed to say. The planet will go on. Isn't this the way of all things? To die, to decay, to become food?

He'd taken an oath, had been bound by blood and loyalty and pain to the president and the nation, but that seemed very distant at that moment.

For a moment, Cade wavered. He felt tired. Tired of protecting humanity. Tired of being tethered to a such a small man. Tired of the fight.

And truth be told, he was tired of this twisted imitation of life. He had sworn never to drink human blood again, an oath he'd made to himself, and he'd left it in the dirt four years earlier alongside a road in Ohio. Since then, he had wallowed in blood. Killed dozens. Told himself he was done pretending to be human, when all he'd really done was let the vampire inside him free.

This seemed like a way out. It seemed almost possible to let it all go.

For a moment, Cade considered letting it win.

CHAPTER TWENTY-TWO

WHILE ZACH WAITED, HE TOOK the plastic wrapper out of his pocket and looked at it in the Laundromat's unhealthy fluorescent light. It had a green logo hand-stamped on the flimsy cellophane.

It said MAGIC MUSHROOMS. There was a little smiling cartoon mushroom. His head was capped with a wizard's starred hat.

He'd seen stuff like this in college. Drug dealers with their own brands, their own special blends, their own trademarks.

Zach figured this was how the infection started and spread. Someone had started using the hallucinogenic mushrooms — because it was a small town, and small towns are boring — and began giving them away to everyone else. And the thing, whatever it was, the intelligence or the fungal creature living in the spores, wormed its way into their brains and turned them into hosts for itself.

It was like the world's most terrifying anti-drug ad. "Kids, stay away from this stuff, or you could become nothing more than a hollow shell for a sentient parasite that intends to destroy the world. And stay in school!"

There was a click on the line. The duty officer was back.

"Mr. Barrows," he said. He sounded hesitant. Scared.

"Still here."

Hesitation. And Zach knew it was over, just by the pause.

"I'm sorry, sir. We cannot authorize the strike."

"Why not?" Zach wasn't sure why it mattered. But he wanted to know.

"The president is asleep, sir. His staff refuses to wake him. He, uh — he's threatened to fire anyone who interrupts his rest."

Zach smiled, despite himself. Wyman. He'd actually expected *Wyman* to come through and save the day.

God, that was stupid.

Zach hung up and sat down on the floor.

The things watching him through the window were still grinning.

But now they started to move toward the door.

CHAPTER TWENTY-THREE

C ADE REMEMBERED SOMETHING.
Zach was still out there. Whatever else he'd done, he'd also made a promise to keep Zach safe. He'd made a promise to the one friend he had, the one bit of humanity he had left.

And he would not fail.

Cade's body began to fight back against the invader.

Everything about Cade was lethal, including his immune system. He felt a roaring in his veins as everything in him responded to the violation, the *insult*, of the thing inside his body and his mind.

Microscopic hunter-killer cells swarmed over the cilia piercing his flesh and bone. His blood turned acidic, its PH balance shifting rapidly, burning out anything foreign.

Cade reached, blindly. He found the tendrils clinging to his head, covering his face.

He took a solid grip. And yanked.

He tore the gripping vines away, tore them out by their roots, felt them coming free of his eyes and nose and mouth and pores.

He crushed the tendrils in his fist, felt them writhe and then die.

He looked at his watch. How long had he been down?

Three minutes to go.

Cade snarled, angry in a way he hadn't felt in a long time. It had distracted him. Almost turned him from his task. Almost convinced him to give up.

Oh, he was going to kill the hell out of this thing.

CHAPTER TWENTY-FOUR

ZACH CHECKED HIS GUN. THE cylinder closed again. It was almost cool to the touch. He had eight small bottles of bleach and eight remaining shells of Dragon's Breath ammo in his pockets.

The door began to open. Zach didn't bother waiting.

He walked across the floor, yanked the door open, and aimed his gun at the infected corpse standing in his way.

It had been a man, probably the bartender or a cook. He wore a once-white apron now scummy with mildew and his eyes were empty and gray.

Zach pulled the trigger, and his head burst into flames, and he fell back into the others behind him.

Zach stepped forward, and fired again. The fire spread among the infected. They staggered away, waving their arms feebly, their clothes burning, skin and bone turning black under the flames.

He'd been hiding in Nebraska for too damn long. If he was going to die now, he was going to die fighting.

CHAPTER TWENTY-FIVE

CADE MOVED THROUGH THE BLAST door leading to the missile silo. The fungus stopped outside the crew cabin, perhaps because there was almost nothing but metal and concrete beyond the door. Nothing worth colonizing.

Cade looked at the missile, towering above him and extending down into the silo below. It was as big as a building. He couldn't break it or dismantle it by hand. His arm still dangled uselessly at the elbow — the bones there still rebuilding themselves. He had no weapons, nothing big enough to cut into the metal skin of the missile, no way to jam the silo doors above.

Behind him, he heard the shuffle of boots on the metal catwalk, the rustle of dry skin against cloth.

One of the dead airmen, moving like a puppet thanks to the parasite inside him.

"You can't stop it now," it said.

As if to punctuate the point, klaxons began to sound and sirens began flashing in the silo. Far above his head, the silo doors began to move to reveal the night sky above. A hollow, mechanical voice boomed from the loudspeakers, hissing and popping as they came to life for the first time in decades.

"SIXTY SECONDS TO IGNITION."

A countdown.

"You can't stop it," the thing wearing the airman's skin said again.

Cade grinned, showing his teeth.

And leaped.

He scrambled up the smooth steel exterior of the missile, headed for the nosecone, one-handed. He stopped near the top, at a riveted panel, and wedged himself against the missile gantry. He reached with his right hand for the missile. His fingers found the thin line where the metal joined, and dug deep.

The panel bent and then tore free of its housing. Cade dropped it and it fell, banging and clanging, down into the depths below.

He peered inside the missile's guts, summoning from memory a diagram of the interior workings of the warhead, the fuel lines, the guidance system.

A hydrogen bomb is actually a very precise instrument. It requires a lens of conventional explosions to slam the fissionable material into a nuclear explosion. Without that exact configuration, a nuclear warhead is mostly just radioactive material on top of a very big rocket.

Cade reached inside the missile and started to pull all those carefully ordered pieces apart.

He heard that flutelike voice scream the word, "*No!*"

Then the dead airman was on him, trying desperately to knock him from his perch, pulling at him with both hands.

Cade was at a disadvantage. He had only one good arm, and he needed it to work. The airman, like the SEALs, was all fiber and dead meat. It wouldn't be easy to fight him, not in this tight space.

"THIRTY SECONDS TO IGNITION," the loudspeaker reminded him.

So Cade decided not to fight. Instead, he simply grabbed something inside the missile and then dropped, falling on top of the airman, sending them both tumbling down toward the bottom of the shaft.

They landed heavily, and hard. Cade used the airman's body to cushion his own fall.

The airman smiled anyway, looking back at Cade with dead grey eyes. That was all the fungus could do. Everything in the body was broken now. It couldn't move.

But it had taken Cade away from the nosecone, and the delicate instruments there.

It smiled because it believed it had won.

"Your time is done," it said to Cade. "It is the way of all things. It is for the best. You will see."

As if to reinforce the point, the loudspeaker began to count down the final ten seconds to ignition.

"TEN... NINE... EIGHT..."

Cade smiled back. Showing his fangs again.

He showed the dead-eyed thing what he was holding in his right hand.

At first, the creature did not understand. Then somewhere in its vast, distributed intelligence, it summoned the memory of one of the human minds it had absorbed, and rifled through the engineering and technical specifications it found there.

It finally recognized the explosive trigger tight in Cade's grip.

It finally realized that Cade didn't want the guidance system. He wanted the warhead's detonator. The size of a softball, it was a small explosive made of standard TNT.

It was nothing compared to the nuclear blast it was supposed to trigger.

But the detonator itself was still a pretty good way to blow things up.

Cade stuffed the small bomb into the mouth of the dead airman just as the creature began to bellow with rage.

"FOUR… THREE… TWO…"

Then Cade leaped for the gantry and was gone before the trigger exploded.

The dead airman's body was vaporized instantly. The explosion also tore a wide hole in the side of the missile's solid-fuel propellant tanks.

The ignition sequence had already started the propellant burning. The fuel exploded, uncontained, out of control.

The missile disintegrated in a massive fireball without ever leaving the silo. Fire and heat shot through the crew cabin, reducing everything in its path to slag and ash.

The fungus — at least this part of it — died screaming, its musical shrieks echoing behind Cade as he ran for the surface.

He still had to find Zach.

CHAPTER TWENTY-SIX

ZACH SAT ON THE STEPS of what appeared to be a Laundromat, a gun in one hand and half-a-dozen dead and burned bodies around him.

Cade approached him cautiously at first.

Zach looked up, then looked past Cade. There was a geyser of flame in the background, a spout of fire from the burning missile silo lighting up the night. The silo's doors were still open, and the fire glowed against the sky. It was almost pretty.

Cade watched Zach's eyes, looking for signs of contagion. They were clear. Normal. His scent was still human.

Good. After all that, Cade would have hated to kill him.

Zach seemed to recognize that he was being assessed. "I'm fine," he said, waving Cade over. "They never touched me. I was out of ammo, then I felt the ground shake, and then I saw the big fire-ball. The rest of them dropped. I guess you won."

Cade sat down next to him on the steps.

"Tactical retreat," Cade said. "I believe it decided to move on to the next battle. There was no point in staying here."

"Terrific," Zach said. "Looking forward to that."

"You're sticking with the job, then?" Cade asked.

"Not sure," Zach said. "I suppose it's up to Wyman."

Cade considered his next words very carefully. He was bound by an oath, after all.

But there were higher loyalties, as well.

"The president does not always need to know what his subordinates are doing to ensure the safety and stability of the country. This can be for his protection, as well as for the general welfare of the nation."

Zach stared at Cade. "Seriously? That doesn't sound like you."

Cade gave his nanosecond smile. "Admittedly, I first heard it from Richard Nixon."

Zach nodded. That made sense. "Then I guess that means it's up to you."

"You have to know: some things have changed."

Zach smirked, like the world was a test and only he knew the answers. Cade didn't miss that. Not at all. "Oh, you mean like you drinking blood again? Yeah, I figured that out a while ago, Cade."

"That's one thing, yes."

Zach looked away. Thinking. Then he turned back to Cade.

"Some things have changed," he said. "But not everything."

He offered Cade his hand.

Cade took it. He felt something he had not felt for a long, long time.

He felt grateful.

EXCERPTS FROM BRIEFING BOOK:

CODENAME: NIGHTMARE PET

APPENDIX A:
Timeline of Events in American History
(Partial)

August 18, 1590
Roanoke Settlement Vanishes
The first English settlement in America disappears, leaving only a cryptic word carved on a tree: "Croatoan." Local Native American legends claim the area is cursed.

1690
Miskatonic University founded as Miskatonic Liberal Seminary.

1692
Salem Witch Trials
Salem, Massachusetts — Two dozen people are hanged, killed, or die in prison after being accused of witchcraft. The accusations begin after Salem residents report seeing a "man in black" who allegedly leads a cult of devil worshippers in the colony.

July 14, 1692
Spectral Invasion of Cape May
Cape May, Massachusetts — Strange beings, seemingly impervious to bullets, attack the settlement, causing the locals to flee into the local military fort for shelter. After two weeks of terrorizing the colonists, they disappear without a trace.

1720

First Freemason Meeting in America, King's Chapel, Boston, Mass.

1735

The birth of the Jersey Devil (date is approximate)

Leeds Point, New Jersey — According to local legend, the Jersey Devil was born to a woman named Mrs. Leeds, who cursed her 13th pregnancy as a devil. The child was born normally, but developed horns, hooves and wings within moments and then escaped out the chimney and into the woods. Sightings continue to this day.

1750

Dr. Thomas Benton born (date is approximate)

1775

The Professor

Philadelphia, Pennsylvania — A mysterious figure, known only as "the Professor," is introduced to George Washington by Benjamin Franklin. He is later central to the drafting of the Declaration of Independence, the design of the U.S. flag, and the Great Seal of the United States. His true identity remains unknown.

1776

Illuminati Founded

Ingolstadt, Bavaria — Adam Weishaupt, professor of law at Ingolstadt University and freemason, founds the Bavarian Order of the Illuminati.

July 4, 1776
Declaration of Independence
The 13 colonies of America declare their independence from Great Britain, beginning the Revolutionary War.

1777
The Washington Prophecy
Valley Forge, Pennsylvania — General George Washington reportedly receives the "Washington Prophecy," a warning from a shadowy figure about the future of the republic.

April 30, 1789 – March 4, 1797
Presidency of George Washington
First president of the United States of America. (See also: Washington Prophecy)

1790
Headless Horseman Incident
Tarry Town, New York — A local school teacher was found murdered and decapitated, reportedly by the spirit of a dead Hessian soldier.

March 4, 1797 – March 4, 1801
Presidency of John Adams

1800
Decatur vs. the Devil
Hanover Iron Works, New Jersey — Commodore Stephen Decatur, while on an inspection tour of a cannonball factory, spots the Jersey Devil. He orders a cannon to fire on the creature. The crea-

ture is hit through the wing but still manages to fly away.

March 4, 1801 – March 4, 1809
Presidency of Thomas Jefferson

Presidency of James Madison
March 4, 1809 – March 4, 1817

1813
Bonaparte and the Devil
Bordentown, New Jersey — While in exile at his American estate, Joseph Bonaparte reportedly encountered the Jersey Devil while hunting.

March 4, 1817 – March 3, 1825
Presidency of James Monroe

March 3, 1825 – March 4, 1829
Presidency of John Quincy Adams

Presidency of Andrew Jackson
March 4, 1829 – March 4, 1837

March 4, 1837 – March 4, 1841
Presidency of Martin Van Buren

April 13, 1838
The Zombie War
New Orleans, Louisiana — Voodoo queens Marie Laveau and Black Cat Mama Coutreaux battle. Reanimated corpses walk the streets of New Orleans, murdering innocent civilians and "voodoo royalty" alike. The war lasts 32 days and only

ends when Coutreaux's husband, Rudolph Coutreaux, is killed and then resurrected with Laveau's
help.

March 4 – April 4, 1841
Presidency of William Henry Harrison

April 4, 1841 – March 4, 1845
Presidency of John Tyler

March 4, 1845 – March 4, 1849
Presidency of James Polk

March 4, 1849 – July 9, 1850
Presidency of Zachary Taylor

1850
The Sabretash Mummy
Baltimore, Maryland — Reported resurrection
of a mummy from the Sabretash Expedition.

July 9, 1850 – March 4, 1853
Presidency of Millard Fillmore

March 4, 1853 – March 4, 1857
Presidency of Franklin Pierce

June 29, 1854
The God Machine
Lynn, Massachusetts — John Murray Spear and
a group of followers activate their mechanical
"New Messiah" to usher in a "new age." Although
unpowered, the device begins to move. It is later
smashed to pieces by a mob.

March 4, 1857 – March 4, 1861
Presidency of James Buchanan

1861 – 1865
The American Civil War

March 4, 1861 – April 15, 1865
Presidency of Abraham Lincoln

April 15, 1865 – March 4, 1869
Presidency of Andrew Johnson

May 23, 1867
"A human vampire and a murderer."
Boston Harbor, Massachusetts — Nathaniel Cade, a young sailor on the whaling vessel *Charlotte*, is turned into a vampire.

September 11, 1867
Cade pardoned
Boston, Massachusetts — Cade is pardoned by President Andrew Johnson in exchange for his service to the United States. Cade is then bound to protect the president and the nation by a blood oath, administered by voodoo priestess Marie Laveau.

December 10, 1867
Baltimore Gun Club Launch
Tampa, Florida — The Baltimore Gun Club, led by its president Impey Barbicane, fires a massive cannon containing a manned cylinder with the aim of reaching the moon.

March 4, 1869 – March 4, 1877
Presidency of Ulysses S. Grant

April 5, 1873
The Bloody Benders
Cherryvale, Kansas — Cade encounters the "Bloody Benders," a family of German immigrants who killed guests at their roadside inn in occult rituals designed to collect blood and souls. (See Appendix B.)

March 4, 1877 – March 4, 1881
Presidency of Rutherford B. Hayes

March 4 – September 19, 1881
Presidency of James Garfield
Died after being shot by Charles Guiteau, a man who claimed he was possessed by demons.

September 19, 1881 – March 4, 1885
Presidency of Chester A. Arthur

March 4, 1885 – March 4, 1889
Presidency of Grover Cleveland

March 1888
Deadman's Hole Incident
Julian, California — Two hunters are attacked by a huge, Sasquatch-like creature and kill it. In its lair, they discover the remains of at least five people missing for years. The body of the creature is displayed to the public at the local police station. It then vanishes from the public record.

March 4, 1889 – March 4, 1893
Presidency of Benjamin Harrison

December 21, 1890
The creation of the Boogeyman entity
Dr. Francis Tumblety performs the rite that will eventually give birth to the entity known as the Boogeyman.

March 4, 1893 – March 4, 1897
Presidency of Grover Cleveland
Only president to be elected to two, non-consecutive terms.

May 1, 1893
Chicago World's Fair
The World's Columbian Exposition opens to the public in Chicago, Illinois. Serial killer H.H. Home used his nearby hotel as a "murder castle" to kill many visitors to the fair.

March 4, 1897 – September 14, 1901
Presidency of William McKinley
Assassinated by Leon Frank Czolgosz.

John Wilkes Booth Dies
Jan 16, 1901
Enid, Oklahoma — John Wilkes Booth, hiding under an assumed name, dies after he is found by Nathaniel Cade.

September 14, 1901 – March 4, 1909
Presidency of Theodore Roosevelt

1903
Roosevelt and the Winchester House
Then-President Theodore Roosevelt tries to visit Sarah Winchester, heiress to the Winchester fortune, at the home she was instructed to build by a fortune-teller to atone for the spirits of all the Native Americans killed by Winchester rifles. Told that she must never stop building the house, the mansion includes 2,000 doors, 160 Rooms, 47 fireplaces, 40 staircases and an unknown number of secret passages. Roosevelt was turned away at the door by a servant, who told him, "The house is not open to strangers." Sarah Winchester died Sept. 5, 1922.

November, 1907
New Orleans Cult Arrests
New Orleans police raid the swamps near the city after a group of squatters is attacked. A hidden cult of over 100 members is found. The object of their worship, a strange, "squid-like" statue, is confiscated.

March 4, 1909 – March 4, 1913
Presidency of William Taft

March 4, 1913 – March 4, 1921
Presidency of Woodrow Wilson

April 6, 1917 – November 11, 1918
World War I

October 31, 1919
Boogeyman Incident
New Orleans, Louisiana — Cade faces the Boogeyman for the first time in its incarnation as "The Axe-Man of New Orleans."

March 4, 1921 – August 2, 1923
Presidency of Warren G. Harding

August 2, 1923
President Harding dies
San Francisco, California — President Warren G. Harding dies suddenly. Suspicion briefly focuses on magician Charles Carter, AKA "Carter the Great," who entertained the president onstage during his act that night. However, federal authorities later say Harding's death was due to natural causes.

August 2, 1923 – March 4, 1929
Presidency of Calvin Coolidge

1925
Child Murders in Red Hook
Red Hook, New York – Authorities investigate a series of child disappearances and murders. The crimes stop suddenly after an old lodge building is demolished.

1927
The Vampire Murders
Providence, Rhode Island -- A series of "vampire murders" reported. Later, local authorities intercept a bootlegger's truck that contains the stolen corpse of Benjamin Franklin. Cade sent to inves-

tigate. Results inconclusive. Possibly related to the Innsmouth incident.

1927
Destruction of Innsmouth
Innsmouth, Massachusetts — The town was discovered by U.S. treasury agents to be populated mostly by hybrid human-sea creatures. Operative Nathaniel Cade leads a mission to clear out the infestation. The town's subsequent destruction was blamed on an out-of-control fire, started by bootleggers. No survivors are found.

1928
Dunwich Creature
Dunwich, Massachusetts — An unknown creature destroyed several homes and killed or injured more than a dozen people before being killed itself by a group of scholars from neighboring Miskatonic University. Possibly related to the Innsmouth incident

March 4, 1929 – March 4, 1933
Presidency of Herbert Hoover

July 2, 1929
The Evangelist Slayings
Detroit, Michigan — Benjamino Evangelista, an Italian immigrant who later renamed himself Benny Evangelist, is gruesomely murdered along with his wife and four children. Evangelist was a real-estate speculator and cult leader rumored to be connected to organized crime. He was killed while working on his book of magic, The Old-

est History of the World as Revealed by Occult Sciences. Witnesses reported strange winds and the shadowy figure of a small man late that night. The crime has never been solved.

1931
Pabodie Expedition Lost
Antarctica — The Pabodie Expedition, sponsored in part by the Nathaniel Derby Pickman Foundation, is wiped out, except for two survivors, after discovering unusual fossils and perfectly preserved corpses of previously unknown animals from millions of years in the past.

March 4, 1933 – April 12, 1945
Presidency of Franklin Roosevelt

Oct 30, 1938
Grover's Mill Intrusion Event
Grover's Mill, New Jersey — Radio broadcast of events is considered to be a hoax.

World War II
December 7, 1941 – December 2, 1945

1943
Cade Meets Konrad
Darmstadt, Germany – Nathaniel Cade encounters Dr. Johann Konrad for the first time. (See: Dr. Johann Konrad Dippel AKA The Baron Von Frankenstein)

April 12, 1945 – January 20, 1953
Presidency of Harry Truman

July 16, 1945
Trinity Atomic Bomb Test

Detonation of the first Atomic Bomb, during which J. Robert Oppenheimer says, "I am become Death, destroyer of worlds," unwittingly completing an ancient ritual.

January 24, 1946
CIA Founded

The Central Intelligence Agency is founded by President Harry S. Truman, who hands a ceremonial black cloak and wooden dagger to Sidney Souers, the agency's first director, unwittingly completing an ancient ritual.

June 14, 1947
Roswell Intrusion Event

Roswell, New Mexico — Wreckage from what is thought to be a spacecraft, including "alien" bodies, is found outside Roswell, New Mexico. The Air Force, after initially confirming the incident, has denied it ever since.

June 24, 1947
Arnold Sighting

Mt. Rainier, Washington — Kenneth Arnold, a businessman and private pilot from Boise, Idaho, sees a group of what he calls "flying saucers" while in the air.

1951
Pabodie II

Antarctica — An expedition is sent to the Arctic

to re-trace the steps of the Pabodie explorers, with the hope of finding some trace of the discoveries left behind. After a brief radio report of finding what appeared to be an alien craft, the expedition lost all contact during a massive storm. No survivors were found.

January 20, 1953 – January 20, 1961
Presidency of Dwight Eisenhower

August 21, 1955
The Kelly Intrusion Event
Hopkinsville, Kentucky — Two families report an encounter with "little green men," described as "goblins" or "gremlins," who appeared in the night and harassed and terrorized them.

1957
"Teenage Monster" Incident
Camden, New Jersey — Another experiment with Konrad's work leads to a local doctor, last name Carlton or Karlton, assembling a creature from the parts of several deceased teenage athletes. After the creature murdered several people, Operative Nathaniel Cade sent to deal with the doctor and his experiment.

January 20, 1961 – November 22, 1963
Presidency of John F. Kennedy

September 16, 1961
Hill Intrusion Event
Groveton, New Hampshire — Betty and Barney Hill report being abducted by sinister "alien"

beings piloting a strange, "bat-winged" aircraft.

November 22, 1963
John F. Kennedy Assassinated

Dallas, Texas — President Kennedy is killed as a result of a conspiracy led by The Shadow Company, a rogue operation working within the United States' intelligence community. The operation is spearheaded by a young agent code-named Graves.

November 22, 1963 – January 20, 1969
Presidency of Lyndon Johnson

April 4, 1968
Martin Luther King Assassinated

Memphis, Tennessee — The Rev. Martin Luther King is assassinated as a result of the Shadow Company's Operation: PREACHER.

June 5, 1968
Robert F. Kennedy Assassinated

Los Angeles, California — Robert Kennedy assassinated as a result of the Shadow Company's Operation: GALAHAD.

1969
Underground Base near Dulce

Construction begins on a massive underground facility near Dulce, New Mexico.

January 20, 1969 – August 9, 1974
Presidency of Richard Nixon

1970
Konrad Recaptured
Biafra/Disputed Provinces of Nigeria – Cade captures Dr. Johann Konrad while the doctor attempts to re-create his *Unmenschsoldaten* project with Soviet sponsorship.

March 1972
The Loveland Frog
Loveland, Ohio — A four-foot tall, manlike frog is spotted by police.

August 9, 1974
President Richard Nixon Resigns
President Richard Nixon resigns in the wake of the Watergate scandal. Cade's cover is nearly blown when Nixon discusses his existence while being taped. The tapes are hastily erased, leading to the famous "18-and-a-half minute gap."

August 9, 1974 – January 20, 1977
Presidency of Gerald Ford

1975
Vampire King Encounter
Jeremiah, Massachusetts — A nest of vampires is discovered in a small New England town after a series of strange murders and reports of a mysterious "sleeping sickness." A King Vampire is suspected of causing the outbreak as part of his attempt to set up "outposts" of his "vampire nation" within the borders of the United States. Operative Cade was sent to the town with the aim of containing the epidemic and terminating the Vampire King.

However, he was ordered back to Washington D.C. on another assignment, and the town was instead burned and removed from the maps. An unknown number of infected individuals escaped.

June 23, 1975
Boogeyman Incident
Ojai, California — Cade encounters and kills the Boogeyman in its incarnation as "The Char-Man."

January 20, 1977 – January 20, 1981
Presidency of Jimmy Carter

1979
Dulce Intrusion Event
Dulce, New Mexico — A battle breaks out between "aliens" and U.S. military personnel at the Archuleta underground base. A routine expansion project reveals a hidden tunnel leading to a nest of unknown humanoid creatures. Operative Nathaniel Cade sent to the facility. No hostiles survive.

1980
Boogeyman Incident
Blairstown, New Jersey – Seven teen counselors at the summer camp on the shore of this resort town were ritually slaughtered by an unknown assailant. The sole survivor, a young woman, was institutionalized after claiming her friends were killed by a former camper, dead for over twenty years.

January 20, 1981 – January 20, 1989
Presidency of Ronald Reagan

March 30, 1981
Reagan Assassination Attempt

Washington, D.C. — John Hinckley Jr. shoots President Ronald Reagan. This leads to a full pardon for Johann Konrad, whose occult surgery techniques are used to save Reagan's life.

May 1981
The Phantom Clowns

Kansas City, Boston, Castle Rock, and other cities — Various cities throughout the United States report a wave of "phantom clown" sightings, where mysterious figures, dressed as clowns, attempted to abduct children in broad daylight. One child reported that the van the clowns drove had a picture of the devil painted on the side. The clowns were never captured. Sightings continue to the present day.

June 29, 1988
The Lizardman of Scape Ore Swamp

Lee County, South Carolina -- A seven-foot-tall reptilian humanoid is reported emerging from the swamp, attacking and chasing witnesses. Despite repeated sightings, it has never been captured. Similar creatures have been seen in Ohio, Florida, British Columbia, and Iowa.

January 20, 1989 – January 20, 1993
Presidency of George H.W. Bush

January 20, 1993 – January 20, 2001
Presidency of Bill Clinton

January 20, 2001 – January 20, 2009
Presidency of George W. Bush

November 29, 2001
Osama Bin Laden Killed
Parachinar, Pakistan — Operative Nathaniel
Cade tracks and kills Osama Bin Laden.

January 20, 2008 – 2012
Presidency of Samuel Curtis

January 14, 2010
White House Attack
Washington D.C. — White House is attacked by
Konrad's *Unmenchsoldaten* in an attempt to kill the
President and break the national spirit. It is stopped
by Nathaniel Cade and his new handler, Zachary
Barrows. Former Special Agent William Hawley
Griffin and 11 Secret Service agents are killed.

April 28, 2011
Snakehead Outbreak
A virus is released that turns humans into strange,
reptilian creatures — similar to the residents of Innsmouth, Massachusetts. (1927). The source is traced
back to Liberty, Iowa, where Operative Nathaniel Cade destroys a Shadow Company operation
before the virus reaches the general population.

September 19, 2012
Boogeyman Incident
Mansfield, Ohio — A Curtis campaign worker
and a volunteer are brutally murdered while in a

compromising position. Scrawled in their blood on the wall of the crime scene: "IT'S GOOD TO BE BACK." Operatives Nathaniel Cade and Zachary Barrows investigate and determine the Boogeyman has returned in a new incarnation, and intends to kill the President of the United States.

APPENDIX B:
CADE VS. THE BLOODY BENDERS

CHERRYVALE, KANSAS, APRIL 5, 1873.

The family placed Cade at the head of the table. He'd arrived at the Wayside Inn outside Cherryvale after sundown. The family was agitated, but not by his presence. There seemed to be a brief debate between the four of them conducted in a guttural language that sounded like German. Cade could hear every word but didn't understand a single one. He made a mental note to himself to begin learning languages. His mind seemed to have an infinite capacity since he was changed and not all of his prey would speak English.

After a few moments, the family patriarch cut off the argument with a firm tone and a chopping motion of his hand. His iron-gray hair and beard gave him the look of an Old Testament prophet delivering the word of God. His wife — or sister, the reports were uncertain — looked unhappy, but her deeply lined face did not appear to do much smiling in any case. The son, a handsome man with slightly addled eyes, did not appear to care one way or another. But there was no mistaking the look of triumph on the fine-boned features of the daughter. Whatever decision the old man had made, it was the one she wanted.

The family was solicitous toward Cade, but only she was talkative. She introduced them all around as they sat for the meal. The old man, her father, was John, she said. Her mother was Kate, who dumped stew onto a plate in front of Cade, her face still set in a frown. The younger man was John Jr. He looked up at his name and started to stand, but his father put him back in his chair with a hard glance.

And the young woman was also named Kate, after her mother. "And your name is Cade," she laughed, putting a hand on his arm. "We'll have to be very specific about who we ask to pass the salt tonight."

Her touch lingered. If Cade still had any attraction to humans, he might have been charmed. She was lovely, possessing as her brother did the finer parts of both her parents without the damage of their years. Or, for that matter, their foul tempers. But it was more than that. Kate had a vitality, an awareness that was missing from the rest of the family. It was as if the younger Kate had access to a hidden spring of life and energy.

Whatever it was, it certainly wasn't the food. Cade looked at the rancid, cold mess on his plate and was thankful he no longer ate.

"You said you were from Washington, Mr. Cade?" Kate asked. "Then you must be well-versed in Spiritualism. Have you any experience with the mysteries of the Other Side?"

"I've heard of it," Cade said.

"It is my great passion," she said. "I am not too modest to say that I have conducted séances and readings for our visitors. I've even lectured at the town hall on the subject. Of course, that caused quite a scandal."

"Really?"

An impish grin came onto her face. "I believe, as many Spiritualists do, that our bodies are not meant to be chained with false morality. Some say this means I believe in wanton and slatternly behavior. Some even called me a witch. But surely we were not given these forms if we were not meant to enjoy them?"

Cade said nothing.

"Perhaps you would allow me to give you a private session?"

Her eyes danced when she said this and Cade knew how previous travelers on this route were distracted.

Without waiting for his answer, she took Cade's hand and held it. The mother grunted and scowled and left the table, taking away plates to the kitchen. The father gave a nearly imperceptible nod to the son, and they both rose and went into another room.

"My, but your hand is cold, Mr. Cade. Perhaps we can do something about that."

She looked at his palm. Her practiced smile faltered. "Your life-line," she said, suddenly uncertain. Whatever she saw in Cade's palm, it was enough to throw her off her practiced script. She recovered quickly, but the confusion was still evident when she looked in Cade's eyes. "Your life-line. Yes. I see a long and prosperous — "

Cade jerked his hand away so quickly it sounded like whip moving through the air. Behind him, he held the large iron hammer that John Jr. had swung, almost silently, toward the back of his head. John Jr., not quite realizing what had happened, struggled mightily with the handle.

Cade kept the hammer in place, as still as a rock. Kate's mouth was open in shock. Cade, with barely a shift in his position, yanked on the hammer and sent John Jr. flying over the table and into the far wall.

Cade turned at the sound of a wailing banshee. Kate's mother came at him from the kitchen, screaming and wielding a knife as long as her forearm.

"Blüt und Seelen! Blüt and Seelen für Mein Meister!"

Cade flipped the hammer in his grip and threw it with pinpoint accuracy. It crushed her skull and snapped her neck in the same instant. Her body was knocked cleanly off its feet.

The patriarch of the clan was not deterred by this. But he wasn't about to make the same mistakes as his wife and son, either. Cade heard the revolver slide free from the leather of the holster hidden under the man's shirt. He kicked at the base of the table and sent it skidding over the wooden floor. It hit the old man at the waist and ran over him like a steam engine.

Kate was still staring, still in her chair.

Cade, still seated as well, turned his gaze back to her.

She regained enough presence of mind to begin a chant. It was not the guttural language they had spoken earlier. It was more glottal, wetter-sounding, a collection of vowels and sibilance tangled together.

Cade felt something gather in the dark with only the first word or two. He didn't give it any more time to develop. His hand went to her throat. She choked and stopped speaking. Cade allowed her just enough air to breathe.

Pulling her along with him, he stood and kicked his chair away. He examined the floor behind him. Cade had smelled death and rot and fear from outside the front door. It was strongest here. His eyes picked out the hairline joins in the boards where the trap door was hidden.

Still holding Kate by the throat, he reached down and lifted the door open. The stink of death hit him like a garden in summer. This was where they had dumped the bodies of all the other travelers after the hammer blows. Many, many bodies. He couldn't separate all the different scents.

John Jr. had recovered enough to gain his feet. He saw his sister — or wife, as the reports had it — in Cade's hand and charged like a bull.

Cade threw the woman at him, sending them both to the floor in a tangle of limbs.

He faced Kate and showed his fangs. The shock, along with the pain in her throat, kept her from repeating her chant.

"*Das Vampir,*" she breathed. "*Blütsauger.*" Her face was a muddle of confusion and pain. "I had hoped — had prayed — We were trying to summon you. But why this? Have we displeased you?"

Cade crossed to her. Her brother groaned. Cade tossed him away like a scrap of trash. Any answers would come from her.

"Tell me who you serve. It was never about the thefts, was it? You sold their goods, but that's not why you killed them. Who were you serving?"

Kate looked even more baffled. "You know. You *must.*"

"I am not who you think I am," Cade said.

Then Kate smiled, just a little. Arrogance shone

through her eyes.

"Someone will succeed where we failed. Someone else will call him. And then — "

She went quiet as Cade got very close to her. "Whatever you meant to summon, you brought me instead. And whoever tries the same will find me as well."

She might have replied, but Cade broke her neck with a backhanded slap.

He made certain the men were dead before gathering the bodies and taking them out of the house. He loaded them onto his wagon. Then he hitched the Benders' horses to their own wagon, already loaded with their stolen goods and possessions. The team needed no encouragement to run when he released them; animals feared Cade instinctively. The horses galloped away, a false lead for anyone who came looking for the family to follow.

He took the family with him in the opposite direction. He'd bury them – and himself – before sunrise, but only he would rise again. No one would ever find them. The Benders would disappear.

True, he could have left them in their gruesome little inn to await the searchers who'd come sooner or later. But his orders were to remove them completely and to give no sign that they'd died. As Kate had confirmed, there were others out there with the same goals as the Benders. Better if those people didn't know what had happened.

Better if the hunters didn't realize they were being hunted themselves.

APPENDIX C:
CRYPTO SAPIENS
A report by the Nightmare Pet Working Group

CRYPTO SAPIENS

Crypto Sapiens is the all-encompassing name given to those creatures, entities and organisms sharing this planet with us but that seem completely alien; that is to say, that cannot be explained by evolution or human agency; that do not appear to conform to observable laws of physics; that appear to be entirely outside our natural world.

In short, Crypto Sapiens refers to the supernatural, and those things that spring from it. They appear to possess some kind of intelligence or to be guided by some kind of intelligent agency. But their aims and motivations are completely unknown to us. Hence the name used in this report: from the Latin words "crypto," for "hidden," and "sapiens," for "wisdom."

Despite all we have learned in the past two centuries of encounters with this hidden intelligence, we still do not know what these beings want, or why. All we can say for certain: we share this planet with an intelligence that is hidden from us, and is indifferent to us at best, and openly hostile at worst.

I. HUMANOIDS
A. Transformed Humans
1. Homo Sapiens Necrosis (The Undead;

Post-mortals)

  a. Vampires

  b. Werewolves

  1. Skinwalkers – Unlike "ordinary" werewolves, these creatures appear to be human only on the surface. They quite literally turn themselves inside-out to reveal the true animal inside, which often looks like a human-sized animal. Folklore says these creatures were human before they were cursed by Native American shamans, but they appear to be entirely bestial, with only rudimentary skills at imitating human beings.

  2. Were-panthers

  3. Jaguarmen

  4. Wendigo/Windigo — Sometimes confused with the Sasquatch folklore, but an entirely different monster altogether, with no question of its malevolence or its hostility toward humans. According to Native American legend, the Wendigo (sometimes Windigo) is a beast-like humanoid who roams the forests of Northern Canada. Formerly human, the Wendigo committed the ultimate sin of feasting on human flesh, usually while lost in the woods. Once this was done, the Wendigo was doomed to continue hunting and eating humans until its curse could be transferred to another unwary traveler. Only then could the beast die, after reverting to human form. The mechanism of the transfer is obscure – some sources state that the Wendigo must be killed and eaten itself, while others maintain that the process is automatic once another lost traveler feeds on his companions.[1]

  c. Reptoids

  1. Innsmouth Families

2. Snakeheads

d. Zombies — There's a great deal of confusion over the term "zombie," which has been applied to all manner of reanimated corpses. The name is actually taken from vodou or voodoo and technically means only a corpse raised from the grave and enslaved by means of the bokor paste. However, casual usage has broadened the name to apply to a number of different creatures and anomalies.

1. Zuvembies (Vodou) — For our purposes, "zuvumbie" refers to the classical vodou manifestation.

2. Walking Dead

i. "Frankensteins" — "Frankensteins" refers to a corpse or assemblage of corpses reanimated by quasi-scientific means (See: Dr. Johann Konrad Dippel AKA The Baron Von Frankenstein). Also known as FrankenSoldiers, *Unmenchsoldaten* or *Todtkrieger.*

ii. Ghouls/ReaniMen -- "Ghoul" refers to the folkloric flesh-eating corpse raised from the dead by occult or other means, while "ReaniMen" refer to the recently deceased raised by scientific accident, intentional effort, or random incident. Both share the taste for living human tissue.

iii. Mummies — "Mummies" is the catch-all term for reanimated corpses raised from Egyptian tombs through ancient curses.

3. Runners

i. Rage Virus Carriers — An unlucky group of animal activists discovered the Rage virus when they tried to free a group of experimental lab animals. Passed in human bodily fluids, immediately capable of breaching the blood-brain barrier, the virus sent the amygdala into overdrive, pumping massive amounts of adrenaline into a carrier, while also completely destroying the parts of the brain capable of regulating aggression, fear and violence. The result was an overclocked human being, able to reach speeds of 30 miles per hour and lift upwards of 600 pounds without pain. However, these strains generally caused the carriers hearts to explode within twenty minutes to an hour. The remaining stragglers burned through their supply of blood sugar so rapidly that they went into hypoglycemic shock and died. The virus did not spread beyond the building.

e. Immortals

1. Dr. Thomas "Doc" Benton

2. Dr. Johann Konrad Dippel AKA The Baron Von Frankenstein — Born 1673 in Frankenstein Castle near Darmstadt, Germany, Dippel was considered a child prodigy, capable of reciting the catechism before the age of five. Sent to school at a young age, he shocked and impressed teachers and other students with his intellect and his arrogance. He mastered seminary lessons by day and dabbled in Tarot readings and divination by night. Dippel was obsessed with mortality, as can be seen in his thesis work, "De Mortis" ("On Death"). Finally, he found his true calling in alchemy, and put all his efforts and fortune into a search for the so-called "Elixir of Life." Once imprisoned for heresy, Dippel's title saved him from greater sanctions when questions were raised about the use of corpses taken from graveyards for his experiments. Records concerning the last years of Dippel's life are sketchy at best. Dippel had spent his father's considerable fortune on his attempts to bottle immortality, allowing his

ancestral home to fall into disrepair. Unsubstantiated reports claim that one of his experiments escaped from the crumbling castle and murdered several people in the nearby village. Dippel was forced to flee, and it is widely assumed he died in 1734, leaving no heir. Castle Frankenstein was allowed to fall into disrepair. However, long after his death, Dippel continued to appear in historical records under a variety of aliases. (For instance, he is believed to be the "Heidelberg doctor" who taught Thomas Benton in 1779.) In World War II, it was confirmed that Dippel had successfully synthesized an immortality serum when he reappeared as a member of the Third Reich's "black science" division. He was captured by Operative Nathaniel Cade but turned over to Soviet forces for trial as part of post-war agreements between the Allied powers. In 1974, Cade again captured Dippel – now using the surname "Konrad" in Biafra. Dippel was released from federal custody in 1981 with a full pardon after performing unspecified medical work for the President of the United States. He violated the terms of this pardon in 2009 by attempting to weaponize corpses for a Middle Eastern terror group. He remains at large.

3. The Comte St. Germain

4. The Wandering Nephites

5. Pre-Lapsarian Survivors

i. Lilith

ii. Cain

iii. Nephilim (AKA The Fallen)

f. Known Unknowns[2]

1. Spring-Heeled Jack

2. The Black Flash of Provincetown

3. The Mad Gasser of Mattoon

4. The Blue Phantom of Route 66

5. Phantom Clowns

6. Phantom Social Workers

7. The Boogeyman (AKA Hook-Hand, the Charman, the Goat-Man, and a variety of other killers from local folkore) — BOOGEYMAN is our code-name for a seemingly unkillable serial murderer who continually eludes any attempt to destroy him. It appears to have a wide variety of psychic and physical abilities, not least of which is the habit of returning to life after massive bodily trauma and, in some case, apparently full dismemberment. Boogeyman simply lives to kill. Cade has engaged the target several times, most recently with an incident near Crystal Lake, New Jersey in 1980. He has never managed to successfully kill or capture the creature. May be related to the other known unknowns, which are all seemingly human but vanish without a trace, and are uniformly sinister and hostile to human life.

B. Humanoid Creatures

1. Ape-men — Also known as the hairy humanoid, the North American Ape, and a variety of other names, these creatures have been spotted throughout human history in every culture and region. Theories vary on what, exactly, they are — whether they are an undiscovered animal, a genetically engineered experiment from alien visitors, or a branch of the human family tree that stayed closer to our roots. Most sightings are relatively peaceful, despite the overwhelming level of terror that witnesses report, along with a strong smell of sulfur. However, a handful of encounters

— usually in conjunction with UFO sightings — tend to be extremely disturbing, if not outright dangerous. In these cases, witnesses report the same feelings of dread, but also receive clear signals of malevolence. The creatures can even be violent or predatory, with several well-known cases ending in attempted child abductions, physical attacks, and at least one death.

   i. Sasquatch ("Bigfoot," "Skunk Ape," "Wild-man," North American Ape-man)

   ii. Yeti (Abominable Snowman, Himalayan Ape-man)

   iii. Orang Pendek ("Little Men," East Asian Ape-man)

   2. Birdmen

   i. Mothman — In 1967, a large, winged human-oid terrified the entire town of Point Pleasant, Virginia, eluding capture despite multiple sight-ings. The town was also visited by MIBs, UFOs, and so-called "aliens" who appeared to groups of contactees. Just as the town was about to descend into complete anarchy, the Silver Bridge collapsed just before Christmas, killing dozens in one of the worst bridge accidents in U.S. history. Since then, Mothman – and other winged humanoids – have been seen all over the world, although never in the same number and intensity as in Point Pleasant. One famous photo even claims that Mothman can be seen flying away from the rubble of the Twin Towers on September 11, 2001.

   ii. Owlman, other birdmen — Similar to Moth-man, these winged beings have been spotted in locations all over the world, including one famous sighting of a human-shaped wingman "swimming" through the air above New York City.[3]

C. Other Terrestrial Species (Cryptoterrestrials)

There is a widespread belief – even among some high-ranking members of government – that the earth has been visited repeatedly by beings from other worlds, who travel in spacecraft commonly referred to as UFOs or Flying Saucers. This is simply untrue. The Earth is, however, home to several non-human species, including one which apparently delights in toying with human beings and which perpetuates the UFO mythology as a cover for its own aims, whatever those may be.

1. "Aliens"

a. Greys/Feys/Sheed

Now seen everywhere in popular culture, the little grey men have become a common symbol of the UFO phenomena. Commonly depicted both in fictional works and by witnesses to actual events as small, gracile and thin in body, with large heads, huge eyes with no pupils and thin, lipless mouths. Fewer people realize, however, that these beings have been sighted throughout human history and given various names. In European cultures, they were known as "little people," "the Fey" or "Fair Folk," or "Fairies," and "The Sidhe" or "Sheed." They were known to capture travelers, take them to their exotic underground lairs and perform experiments that would be familiar to anyone who's read any alien abduction tales. Sometimes the abductees would be returned to tell the story. Other times, only those who escaped would be able to warn others. In the twentieth century, the Greys/Feys/Sheed became more overt as they perpetuated the UFO myth. In several cases, they attempted to intrude upon our human world from their own. (SEE: Hopkinsville, Dulce, et al.) They appear to have the innate ability to alter human perception – possibly at an electromagnetic level which disrupts neural function and memory – which enables them to give the impression of having much greater technologies and abilities. Their true agenda is unknown. However, given the violent, cruel and often fatal actions suffered by their victims, they must be considered firmly on The Other Side despite occasional protests of benevolence to humanity.

b. Reptilians

Not to be confused with Reptoids (See: Homo Sapiens Necrosis: Reptoids), these are intelligent, non-human creatures who, like the Grey/Fey/Sheed, use the UFO mythology as a cover story for their presence on Earth. They alternately claim – when they do speak to humans – to be fighting the Greys or working with them. Some claim ancestry from a planet circling a star in the Draco constellation. However, as with the Greys, their presence in human folklore goes back long before any tales of space travel or alien craft. Their agenda is more definitively sinister: the association of the serpent with evil across cultures can be traced back to mythical encounters with "Serpent People" who have acted as enemies to humanity. Ancient heroes have been credited with battling and defeating these Serpent People, thus enabling human civilization to flourish. Their numbers appear to be diminished – sightings are rare compared to Greys (and indeed, to the more feral Reptoids or any other Cryptoterrestrials.)

ENDNOTES

[1] Though some members of the working group argued for the inclusion of the Wendigo (also known as the Windigo, depending on the source) in the category of "Ape-Men," it was decided, after some debate, that the Wendigo is more accurately categorized as a were-beast. According to legend, a man transforms into an inhuman, ape-like, feral creature driven by a hunger for human flesh after he succumbs to cannibalism while stranded in the wild. Appropriately, this is not an offshoot of the human evolutionary tree, but rather a man transformed by forces unknown into a post-mortal creature.

[2] Obviously, much of this classification system is a work-in-progress, as the group assembles data from a wide range of sources, most of it with limited degrees of accuracy. Until verifiable evidence is presented, some phenomena, sadly, will have to be classified in this "other" category, which is a catch-all for those beings and creatures who cannot be assigned definitive places in this taxonomy.

[3] "An Aerial Mystery," New York Times, Sept. 12, 1880.

ABOUT THE AUTHOR

CHRISTOPHER FARNSWORTH IS A NOV-ELIST, screenwriter, and journalist. He is the author of *Flashmob*, *Killfile*, *The Eternal World*, and the President's Vampire series: *Blood Oath*; *The President's Vampire*; *Red, White, And Blood*; and *The Burning Men*. He's also written the comic book *24: Legacy: Rules of Engagement* for IDW Publishing. His books have been translated into nine languages, published in more than a dozen countries, and optioned for film and television. His work has been published by the *Los Angeles Times*, the *New York Post*, *The Awl*, and *The New Republic*. He lives in Los Angeles with his wife and daughters.

You can find out more at:
www.christopherfarnsworth.com or follow him on Facebook at:
www.facebook.com/AuthorChrisFarnsworth or on Twitter at: *@chrisfarnsworth*.

Made in the USA
Middletown, DE
20 March 2021